"I have another statement that's been prepared for your trust, Mr. Foley."

Chance started to correct Poppy's *Mr. Foley* again, but the rest of her words quickly sunk in. "What do you mean 'my trust'?"

"I mean, your late brother and sister-in-law have put funds into a trust for you, as well."

He said nothing, only gazed back at Poppy, confused as hell.

"The children's trust will begin to gradually revert to them when they reach the age of twenty-two," she continued. "That's when the funds in your trust will become available."

Out of nowhere, a thought popped up in the back of Chance's brain. Something he hadn't thought about for a long time—a wish he'd made on a comet when he was fifteen years old. A wish, legend said, that should be coming true about now, since Endicott had been celebrating the "Welcome Back, Bob" comet festival for a few weeks.

He eyed Poppy warily. "H-how much money is in that trust?"

Her captivating green eyes had never looked more serious. "A million dollars, Mr. Foley. Once the children reach the age of twenty-two, that million dollars will be yours."

Dear Reader,

When he was fifteen, Chance Foley wished upon a legendary comet for a million dollars. But as the saying goes, "Be careful what you wish for." Although Comet Bob has indeed granted his wish, the fortune comes with strings—a niece and nephew, two diabolical little scamps, that Chance never knew he had. Thank the stars he has the delectable Poppy Digby to help him out.

Poppy, however, is adamant she's only in small town Endicott long enough to deliver the little monsters—ah, she means *children*—to their uncle. Her big life in the big city is too full of big things she needs to get done. She doesn't care how sexy and sweet Chance is. But Comet Bob, the trickster, has plans for Poppy, too.

Thanks for picking up the first book in my Lucky Stars trilogy. I hope you have as much fun reading about Chance and Poppy as I had writing about them. And I hope all your wishes come true!

Happy reading,

Elizabeth

Be Careful
What You Wish For

———

ELIZABETH BEVARLY

HARLEQUIN
SPECIAL
EDITION

ISBN-13: 978-1-335-72411-3

Be Careful What You Wish For

Copyright © 2022 by Elizabeth Bevarly

Harlequin Enterprises ULC
22 Adelaide St. West, 41st Floor
Toronto, Ontario M5H 4E3, Canada
www.Harlequin.com

Printed in U.S.A.

Elizabeth Bevarly is the award-winning *New York Times* bestselling author of more than seventy books, novellas and screenplays. Although she has called places like San Juan, Puerto Rico, and Haddonfield, New Jersey, home, she's now happily settled back in her native Kentucky with her husband and son. When she's not writing, she's binge-watching documentaries on Netflix, spending too much time on Reddit or making soup out of whatever she finds in the freezer. Visit her at elizabethbevarly.com for news about current and upcoming projects; book, music and film recommendations; recipes; and lots of other fun stuff.

Books by Elizabeth Bevarly

Harlequin Desire

Taming the Prince
Taming the Beastly M.D.
Married to His Business
The Billionaire Gets His Way
My Fair Billionaire
Caught in the Billionaire's Embrace

Accidental Heirs

Only on His Terms
A CEO in Her Stocking
The Pregnancy Affair
A Beauty for the Billionaire
Baby in the Making

Visit the Author Profile page
at Harlequin.com for more titles.

For Gail Chasan,
Bob's second best friend (I claim first!).
Thanks for twenty-five years (!) of comet love.

Prologue

"This is lame."

"Says you. The food is awesome."

"Holy crow, who paints a ceiling like that?"

Fifteen-year-old Chance Foley tugged at his necktie for the billionth time and gazed at his three companions sitting on the other side of the table at the Galaxy Ball. His brother, Logan, had naturally been the one to complain, because Logan, at nineteen, complained about everything and thought he was better than everyone else. Certainly better than the three fifteen-year-olds their mother had made him promise to keep an eye on tonight. Chance's friend Felix Suarez was shoveling his dessert into his mouth like it was the last bite of food he'd ever get, even though he lived above his grandmother's restaurant. And his other friend Max Travers, whose hand-me-down suit fitted him even worse than Logan's hand-me-down fitted Chance, was staring at the high ceiling overhead, fascinated.

Chance looked up, too. Max had a point. Although the whole ballroom of Mrs. Pendleton Barclay's estate was pretty gnarly, the ceiling was super trippy. Bright blue and dotted with stars, there was a giant sun and moon in the middle surrounded by cartoon renditions of all the planets. And streaking through the middle of them was a comet. Comet Bob. It actually had a more official handle, the name of the Eastern European scientist who had discovered him, but that name had more consonants than vowels and more syllables than anyone was comfortable with, so Comet Bob it was.

It was the whole reason for the party tonight. Mrs. Barclay's Galaxy Ball was the final event of the monthlong Welcome Back Bob Comet Festival that the small southern Indiana town of Endicott hosted every fifteen years. Comet Bob came back to Earth every fifteen years, always during the third week of September, and he always made his closest pass to the planet at coordinates that were directly above Endicott. It was an anomaly scientists had been trying to explain for generations, but meanwhile the little town had come to claim it as their own.

"I think the ceiling's dope," Chance said. "It would be cool to live in a place like this."

Not that it would ever be in the cards for the Foleys. His dad had been killed by a drunk driver when Chance was twelve, and his mother was newly recovered from a bout with cancer that had dumped the family into medical debt they weren't likely to ever crawl out from under. But Chance didn't care about the money. He was just glad his mom was okay. Hell, if he had to work his part-time job at the boatyard for the rest of his life to help pay off her medical bills, he would.

"Mrs. Barclay is such a weirdo," Logan said.

"I think she's nice," Chance told him. "Not many rich old ladies would invite a bunch of fifteen-year-olds to a house like this."

Then again, Chance and his friends—and all the other fifteen-year-olds at the party tonight—weren't just any fifteen-year-olds. They'd all been born the last year Bob came around. In Endicott, you didn't get much more prestige than being born in a year of the comet. Too bad it didn't bring riches, too.

It could, though. Maybe. A lot of folklore had risen up around Comet Bob over the years. Like the bit about making wishes. Legend had it that if someone in Endicott was born in a year of the comet, and if that person made a wish when Bob came back, then that wish would come true when Bob returned next time. So late last night, when the comet was directly overhead, Chance had sent his wish skyward—a wish for a million dollars. He didn't care if it took fifteen years for it to come true. His mom would have barely made a dent in her medical bills by then. A million bucks, he was sure, could pay off whatever was left. Then he and his mom and his brother could put the whole terrible ordeal of her illness behind them forever.

"Hey, did you guys make a wish last night?" he asked his friends. "I did."

His friends exchanged an anxious glance.

"Um, yeah. Okay. I guess I did, too," Felix confessed.

Max exhaled a defeated sound. "All right. Fine. I did, too."

"Wishes?" Logan asked incredulously. "You guys actually made *wishes* when Bob passed overhead?"

"Shh," Max shot back. "Will you please keep it down? The wishes may not come true if other people hear, even if we were all born in the last year of the comet."

Logan shook his head at the three younger guys. "Incredible. Just what the hell did you wish for?"

Max dropped his glance to his lap. "I wished

Marcy Hanlon would see me as something other than the lawn boy."

Chance bit back a smile. The worst-kept secret at Endicott High School was Max's unrequited love for Marcy, whose family was so rich and so much higher on the social ladder than practically anyone in Indiana he might as well have been pining for a Greek goddess. *Good luck filling that wish, Bob.*

"I wished for a million dollars," Chance offered readily. He didn't care if anyone knew what he wished for. It was a legit request.

Felix added, "And I wished that, just once, something interesting would happen in this town."

Oh, sure. That was even less likely to happen than Marcy Hanlon seeing Max as something other than the lawn boy. Comet festivals aside, nothing interesting ever happened in Endicott.

Chance was about to say something else, but a blonde lady at the next table suddenly turned around and smiled at them. "Be careful what you wish for, boys," she said. She took the hand of the dark-haired man sitting beside her. "Because you know…you might just get it."

They both smiled as they stood up and walked toward the ballroom exit. For some reason, as he watched them go, Chance couldn't quite shake the idea that whoever the lady was, she was a comet kid, too, and Bob had done right by her this year and granted her wish.

It was a good sign. Maybe in fifteen years he really would have a million bucks dropped into his lap. Maybe, somehow, the next time Bob came around, he really would make Chance's wish come true.

Chapter One

Fifteen years later

Chance Foley concentrated hard on unclenching his fists, breathing slowly and reminding himself again that 10:00 a.m. was too early in the day to start drinking. September was turning out to be one hell of a month, and it was barely half over.

It had started on day one, when his beloved vintage Jeep Cherokee rolled into the Ohio River while he and his friend Max were trying to secure his other friend Felix's boat onto its trailer. But the news he'd received three days ago had topped even that. He'd learned that his brother, Logan, whom he hadn't seen or heard from for more than a decade, had died—along with a wife Chance never knew he had—in a freak avalanche while snowboarding in Austria.

One of the many things troubling him at the moment was the realization that he was probably going to miss his Jeep more than he was going to miss his brother. Even before he and Logan had become estranged, they'd never been especially close. That was partly due to the four-year gap in their ages, but also due to the fact that Logan had grown into a typically self-absorbed teenager and never really considered his little brother to be much more than a pest. The only thing Chance knew for sure right now was that Logan and his wife, Adele, had left behind two little kids, six-year-old twins Chance had never known about, either.

Six-year-old twins who were about to become his wards.

"Mr. Foley?"

Chance snapped up his head to look at the tidy, buttoned-down man sitting behind the reception desk of Novak and Hamza, attorneys-at-law. Lionel Abernathy—he'd introduced himself upon Chance's arrival earlier. And never in his life had Chance met someone whose name seemed to match his demeanor more perfectly.

"Yes?" Chance replied.

"I'm sorry for your wait. Ms. Digby just texted. She's on her way now and should be here anytime with the children."

The *Ms. Digby* Lionel was referring to was a Boston attorney who would be meeting with Chance this morning to introduce him to his niece and nephew and go over the particulars of his brother's will.

"Thanks," Chance replied.

Lionel hesitated. "I take it you haven't met them yet?"

Chance shook his head. "No. Ms. Digby said they'd be getting in too late yesterday to arrange a meeting. Have you met them?"

The receptionist nodded. "I picked them up at the airport in Louisville last night to drop off a company car for Ms. Digby to use while she's here in Endicott. The children are, um… They're just, ah, just delightful."

The way he stumbled over the last word gave Chance pause. He opened his mouth to say something else, but Lionel hastily offered, "Can I get you anything? Coffee? Bottle of water?"

Chance shook his head. "No. Thanks. I'm good."

"I'm sure Ms. Digby will only be a few more minutes." He threw Chance a thin smile, then went back to his work.

Chance ran both hands through his dark hair and leaned back in his chair. He wished he'd had time for a haircut—he was long overdue—and he felt weirdly overdressed in simple khakis and a white oxford shirt. He couldn't remember the last time he'd worn these clothes. But they were the dressiest he owned, and he'd felt like he needed to make the best impression possible. His only interaction with Poppy Digby so far had been through emails, and in those she hadn't sounded anywhere near as fun and lighthearted as her name would suggest. She'd been matter-of-fact and straight-to-the-point about everything, using the sort of language that was probably supposed to be comforting—but not really—and doing her best to be reassuring—which she didn't quite manage.

The dichotomy between her bubbly name and her sober email demeanor had made Chance curious enough to google her. But that hadn't helped at all, because in every picture he'd seen of her, she looked like a pin-striped pixie, something that just added to the puzzle. Her bio on the website of the Boston law firm where she worked had been even less helpful, telling him little more about her than her educational and professional credentials. Which, yeah, were impressive, but they still didn't seem to suit her. Not a word about her interests or what she might do for entertainment, which were normally included in a lot of professional profiles. Unless maybe the part about how she spent her spare time reading biographies of economists and pursuing an interest in cacti was supposed to cover that.

All Chance knew for sure about her was that she was bringing his niece and nephew, Quinn and Finn—*Seriously, Logan? You had to give them names like that?*—to her firm's sister law office here in Endicott, and they'd be arriving this morning at 9:30 a.m. sharp. That had been twenty-five minutes ago. Tardiness was another thing that didn't seem to fit Poppy Digby. It only added to the surreal quality of his own life at the moment.

Two kids. Chance was going to be responsible for raising two kids. What the hell had Logan and his wife been thinking to name him as their preferred choice of guardian for their children? There had to have been dozens of people in their current lives who would be more familiar to the kids and better prepared to take on a task like that.

It was hard not to be angry at his brother for not telling him. For six years, Chance could have been the fun uncle, mailing off Christmas gifts and cash-stuffed birthday cards to the next generation of Foleys. Having the kids visit every summer to get to know them better, or flying up to Boston himself once in a while to let them show him their favorite places to visit in their hometown.

But no. Logan had left Endicott to make his way in the world when Chance was sixteen, barely a

week after they buried their mother. It evidently
never occurred to him that leaving behind a minor
brother might be a bit problematic for said minor
brother. Chance had spent the next year and a half
couch surfing with Felix and Max, whose families
had been kind enough to take him in, until he could
sign a lease on his own place when he turned eigh-
teen. Life hadn't exactly gotten easier after that, but
he'd had a good job at the boatyard and a gift for
carpentry, inherited from his father, that had led to
his learning the craft of boatbuilding. Not that there
was a lot of that going on these days, but there was
enough, along with the more regular income from
his marine repair shop, for him to keep himself fed
and clothed and housed and still put a little away
every month for the future.

Of course, now he was going to have two more
people to feed and clothe and house. Quinn and
Finn. *Seriously, Logan? Seriously?* Two people he
knew nothing about and who in turn knew nothing
of him. Two people he was going to be responsible
for for the next god knew how many years. He'd
have to enroll them in school and become a member of the PTA. Cook regular nutritious meals for
them. Keep tabs on what they watched on TV and
what games they played and make sure they were
home before dark.

Was Quinn a typical little girl? Did she like glitter and unicorns and all things pink? Or was she more into bugs and skateboards and mud pies? Maybe Finn was the one into glitter and unicorns and all things pink. Maybe neither of them was. Maybe they were both empty vessels hungry for knowledge. In which case, Chance was really in trouble, because pretty much the only thing he knew about was boats.

He heard a door open and close somewhere down the hall, followed by the heavy *clack-clack-clack* of sensible heels and the softer scuff of rubber-soled sneakers. Ms. Digby and the children had arrived.

The knot in his stomach clenched tighter. He heard another door open and close, the mumble of voices both old and young, and then the law office was silent again. Until a moment later when, out of nowhere, a high-pitched scream split the air of the reception room, followed immediately by the crash of something that sounded really, really expensive. Lionel heard it, too, his previously polite expression rocketing to panic.

"What was that?" Chance asked.

"I guess I should go check," Lionel replied.

He stood and strode down a hallway to his left. Chance heard a door open again, then another scream—this one less high-pitched and more wild-animal sounding—followed by the thump of what could have been a baseball, a book or a body part.

"Ms. Digby!" The receptionist cried out in a way that sounded so, so not good. "That was Ms. Novak's Vander Award! It's Baccarat crystal!"

"Lionel," Ms. Digby replied in a voice Chance could tell she was struggling to keep even. "Do you mind keeping an eye on the children for a few minutes while I talk to Mr. Foley?"

Lionel muttered something in a strangled voice that sounded a lot like, *Are you out of your effing mind?*

Whoa, Lionel, WTF? There are children present. You seemed so professional. Not cool, dude.

"Give Finn your phone," Chance heard Ms. Digby tell Lionel.

"Oh, I don't *think* so."

"The children's devices were all packed by mistake," Ms. Digby explained, "and they become distracted easily. I assume you have some sort of app on your phone that will keep Finn occupied. Quinn has very much enjoyed What's That Cactus? on mine."

"No," Lionel said decisively.

"I'll buy you a new one."

That seemed to give Lionel pause. "What kind?"

"Whatever kind you want."

Lionel immediately named one in the two-thousand-dollar range. Chance knew that because he'd recently priced new phones for himself and had laughed himself silly when he saw the cost of that model.

That didn't seem to deter Ms. Digby, however. "Done. Now give Finn your phone. Quinn already has mine."

Chance heard her clack a few steps toward the waiting room, and then she stopped. "And, Lionel."

"Yes, Ms. Digby?"

"Do not take your eyes off those children for a moment."

Chance told himself he only imagined an audible gulp from the receptionist. "Yes, Ms. Digby."

Clack-clack-clack-clack-clack. Ms. Digby entered the reception room in a way that might have been imperious had it not been for her appearance. She was, in fact, wearing pinstripes—a slender skirt and double-breasted jacket in no-nonsense navy—but the former was splattered with what looked like the better part of a milkshake, and the latter was hanging haphazardly open over a wrinkled blouse and crooked string of pearls. Her short dark hair, so perfectly styled in the photos he'd seen, was sticking straight up in a couple of places, and her round tortoiseshell glasses were askew.

She managed to straighten those glasses—mostly—as she approached, her gaze steady and confident when it met his, her eyes the clearest pale green Chance had ever seen. Green, too, was a splotch of something on her chin, just below her slightly smudged red lipstick. He'd been with Max often enough when the other man ordered one of those matcha drinks at Julie's Java Joint to suspect it was a remnant of one of those.

"Mr. Foley," she said as she switched a leather briefcase from her right hand to her left and extended the former confidently toward him. Automatically, Chance shook it. She had a solid grip, he'd give her that. "Please accept my condolences for the loss of your brother and sister-in-law."

"Thanks," he replied automatically. Her voice was as intriguing as the rest of her, deep and kind of husky for a woman, especially one her size. Which, even wearing sensible heels, was a good six inches shy of Chance's six-one.

"I know you're anxious to meet your niece and nephew," she continued, "but it would be helpful if you and I could have a moment to speak in private first about your brother and sister-in-law's wishes."

"Okay," he said. Truth be told, he didn't mind stalling for a little while longer. He was still kind of, oh, terrified about the prospect of becoming a guardian.

"If you'll follow me?"

She was turning around before she finished to head down a hallway opposite the one from which she'd come. Because it was a Sunday, the offices were empty. Lionel had probably only come in to unlock the place for Ms. Digby.

She led Chance to a room that was plain and functional, a run-of-the-mill meeting room as opposed to someone's office. A long table bisected the space with a dozen chairs surrounding it. She took a seat near the head, gestured at the one across from her for Chance, then slung her briefcase up on the table.

He sat down, and as she withdrew some documents from her bag and began to sort through them, he looked out the bank of windows behind her. The Old Town part of Endicott, where the law office was located, sat on a hill that looked out over the Ohio and an especially green part of Kentucky on the other side. It was a gorgeous day, the sky blue and clear, a soft breeze rippling the trees. Between the law office and the river, the town descended into tidy homes along tree-lined streets, then to a good-sized marina where all manner of watercraft bobbed and tugged at their moorings. Even more boats dotted the river beyond. On any other Sunday like this, Chance would have been right out there with them in the vintage runabout he'd rebuilt from near scratch. There was nothing he loved more than being on the water.

"Now then, Mr. Foley—"

"Call me Chance," he interrupted gently. He

was never comfortable when people called him *Mr. Foley* more than once.

Ms. Digby—Poppy, he corrected himself, since he didn't like using honorifics for other people, either—looked like she wanted to call him Mr. Foley even more emphatically.

"How much do you know about your brother's situation?" she asked.

"Only what I was told by the cops who showed up at my door a few days ago to tell me about the accident and what you told me in your emails after that."

She nodded. "And you mentioned you didn't even know he was married with children."

"No, I didn't even know where he was before you contacted me about his will. And the part about him having a will—not to mention including me in it—almost surprised me more than the part about him having a family."

"Why would that surprise you?"

"Because neither of us is…was…the planning type. No one in my family was. We never had enough to worry about the future."

"Don't you have a will now?" she asked.

He shook his head. "It's never seemed necessary."

"Don't you want to provide for your loved ones after you're gone?"

"I don't have any loved ones to provide for," he said simply.

Her expression changed, and it made something inside Chance twist tight. It had been a long time since anyone had felt sad for him. That a total stranger would be now… Well, it made Poppy Digby seem like a lot less of a stranger.

"I guess now that I'll be caring for Quinn and Finn, I should get a will made up," he said.

She nodded. "I can arrange for someone here at Novak and Hamza to contact you."

"Thanks," he said.

She glanced down at the papers on the table again. "Now then, Mr. Foley…"

"Chance."

She looked up at him again and again didn't follow his request. "As I mentioned in my email, Logan and Adele took care of their children's financial needs. Quinn and Finn have a trust fund that will cover whatever expenses are incurred while they're growing up, including college, weddings, and anything else that might arise. You'll receive a monthly stipend from that trust that will cover their day-to-day needs."

Chance had been surprised when he'd read that in the email. But he'd also been relieved. His folks had had to skimp on a lot when he and Logan were growing up, and they'd often had to go without.

He was glad that wouldn't be the case for his niece and nephew.

"And your brother took your needs into consideration, as well," Poppy continued.

Chance couldn't quite help the surprised sound that escaped him. He'd just never known his older brother to care about anyone but himself. Logan must have done a lot of growing up after he left town.

"You sound doubtful, Mr. Foley."

"Chance."

"Mr. Foley. But Logan and Adele wanted to ensure that the children *and* you have everything you need." She slid a sheet of paper across the table toward him. "This is an assessment of the children's trust fund. I'll send an updated copy to you quarterly, since I and my firm are the children's trustees."

Instead of looking at the paper, Chance sat forward. "You personally are the children's trustee?"

"Yes, though my firm will also be overseeing the administration of the trust. I'm not an estate attorney. I practice corporate law."

"So if you personally are a trustee, did you know my brother?"

Another shadow of melancholy flashed over her green eyes. "Yes. But I knew his wife better. Adele was my cousin."

"Oh. Wow," Chance said. "I'm so sorry. Please accept my condolences for your loss, too."

"Thank you."

He wanted to ask if the two of them had been close, but he could tell just by looking at her that they had been. So he instead looked down at the trust statement. It pretty much went without saying that he'd never seen one before and had no idea what he was looking at, other than a lot of columns with words and numbers. Words like *assets* and *liabilities* and *fund equity* and numbers that had way more digits to the left of the decimal point than made sense.

"I don't understand what I'm looking at," he said.

She pulled herself out of her thoughts and went back to being the no-nonsense attorney from her emails. Well, except for the sticking-up hair and the smudged lipstick. And the fact that she felt less like a stranger than she had before.

"It's what's currently in the children's trust. The rest of your brother's estate will be in probate for now." She passed another piece of paper across the table. "This is a list of your brother's current assets outside the trust. Essentially, all of this will be added to the other funds at some point."

Chance looked at those figures, too. Like the others, they were way too big to belong to a guy who'd left Endicott with nothing but a couple hundred bucks and a used Kawasaki.

He looked up at Poppy. "But this makes it look like Logan had hundreds of millions of dollars in assets."

She held his gaze steadily with those bottle green eyes, and something in the pit of Chance's stomach caught fire. "That's because, when he died, your brother had hundreds of millions of dollars in assets."

Chance's eyebrows shot up to nearly his hairline. "How did Logan come by hundreds of millions of dollars?"

"Logan was working for a tech firm in Boston when—"

"Wait—what?" he interrupted again. "Logan worked for a tech firm?"

Although his brother had taught himself to code when he was still in middle school, and he'd been a good hacker of the dirty tricks variety when they were teenagers, Chance couldn't see him ever living the cubicle lifestyle for a steady paycheck.

"Yes," Poppy said. "And he developed a computer program several years ago that allowed companies to legally plunder and sell all kinds of personal information and online habits of anyone who used their websites. It goes without saying that it was worth a gold mine to corporate America. And corporate America paid your brother a gold mine for it."

Okay, that did actually sound like something Logan would have been able to do. Chance probably shouldn't have been surprised that his brother would turn his gift for hacking into making a pile of money.

Poppy pulled another piece of paper from the collection in front of her. "I have another statement that's been prepared for your trust, Mr. Foley."

He started to correct Poppy's *Mr. Foley* again, but the other part of her statement sank in too quickly. "What do you mean my trust?"

"I mean your brother and sister-in-law have put funds into a trust for you, as well."

He didn't know what to say. So he said nothing, only gazed back at Poppy, confused as hell.

When he said nothing, she continued, "The children's trust will begin to gradually revert to them when they reach the age of twenty-two. That's when the funds in your trust will revert entirely to you."

Out of nowhere, a thought popped up in the back of Chance's brain, and he was reminded of something he hadn't thought about for a long time—a wish he'd made to a comet when he was fifteen years old. A wish, legend said, that should be coming true about now, since Endicott had been celebrating the Welcome Back Bob Comet Festival for a few weeks. Something cool and unpleasant wedged in his throat at the memory.

He eyed Poppy warily. "H-how much money is in that trust?"

Her captivating green eyes had never looked more serious. "A million dollars, Mr. Foley. Once the children have reached the age of twenty-two, that million dollars will be yours."

Chapter Two

Poppy Digby waited to see how Chance Foley would react to the news she'd just dumped in his lap. But he only sat motionless, staring back at her, with the dreamiest gray eyes she'd ever seen in her life, all dark and hooded and sultry, the kind of eyes a woman could lose herself in completely.

She shoved her lascivious thoughts to the back of her brain and made herself focus on the reason she was here.

She still couldn't believe he hadn't known his brother's whereabouts for fourteen years. Poppy hadn't known Logan as well as she knew her cousin, of course, but she'd known him well enough, at least while he and Adele were dating and during the early years of their marriage. Maybe she hadn't seen much of the two of them lately—for the past four or five years, she'd been busy clawing her way up the corporate ladder—but when she *had* known Logan, he'd mentioned having a brother often enough that Poppy had assumed the two of them had a normal, if geographically distant, sibling relationship. To discover now that Chance hadn't even known of the children's existence until a few days ago, never mind that he was going to become their custodian…

Oh, this wasn't good. Even when it wasn't unexpected, the sudden fostering of a child could create a difficult situation. And the fostering of the Foley children was going to create a situation that brought a whole new meaning to the term *nuclear family.* Because the Foley children, Poppy had discovered over the past few days, weren't typical children. In fact, she was beginning to suspect they weren't children at all, but were instead feral wolverines dressed as children. Poppy had done little else than try to keep them from wreaking havoc on everything within arm's length. They just didn't know the meaning of the word *no.* Or the word *stop.* Or the words *oh, my god, where did you get that hammer, do you know how much I had to put down for a damage deposit on this place?*

But that was what happened when people—

namely Adele and Logan Foley—first spoiled their children rotten, then turned their children's upbringing over to a string of even more overly indulgent nannies, none of whom ever stayed in the children's lives for more than a few months. Because spoiling and overindulgence of children with no discipline to speak of turned said children into feral wolverines. Logan and Adele had both come from meager backgrounds, and when his sudden riches appeared practically overnight, they'd gone overboard, buying everything they could to make themselves and their children happy. They'd quit their jobs and spent their lives jet-setting around the globe to do all the things neither of them had been able to do before, with au pairs for the kids, who were instructed to give the little tykes anything they wanted and to never ever curb their children's desires or impulses.

The last few days had been nothing but chaos. In addition to being confused about and bereaved by the loss of their parents, the children were undisciplined and screaming for attention—often literally. Poppy had done her best to first indulge them, then supervise them, then restrain them, but none of those things had been possible.

"I'm sure you must have some questions, Mr. Foley," she said.

"Chance," he corrected her. Again.

Not that Poppy was going to be corrected. She

never spoke to clients so familiarly. She and Chance Foley would be a part of each other's lives, professionally speaking, for the next decade or two. Therefore, it was essential that Poppy never *ever* think of him as *Chance*. Doing so could potentially take their relationship beyond the professional. And Poppy simply could not have any relationships in her life right now that weren't professional.

"I have so many questions," Chance said, "that I don't even know where to begin."

Poppy had lots of questions, too. But most of them were about Chance and his own history and life views and whether he preferred boxers or briefs, so it was probably best to just let him drive the conversation for now.

Finally, he asked, "How long will you be in town?"

Of all the questions she'd expected him to ask, that one wasn't even on the long list. "I have a flight back to Boston tonight," she said.

His state of confusion turned to one of alarm. "That soon?"

"I have to get back to work as soon as possible," she told him. "I have a very important case I'll be trying in a little over a week, and I still have a lot of preparing to do. I've been away from work too long as it is."

"But there's still so much we need to talk about."

"Which is why we're sitting here now," she pointed out.

"But…"

He studied her in silence for another moment with those dark, dreamy eyes, and Poppy did her best to withstand the tidal wave of temptation that barreled toward her. Then he threw her a smile, and she was diving headfirst into the wave. Eyes like his had always gotten Poppy into trouble.

"Any chance you could stay a few days longer?" he asked. "Maybe help me get acclimated to the kids?"

Inescapably, she felt herself pulled into the smoky depths of Chance's eyes again. She marveled at the sculpted cheekbones, noted how his bottom lip was just the tiniest bit fuller than the top. She heard his voice echoing in her ears, so smooth and strong. She inhaled the scent of him from across the table, something clean and earthy and raw. And, oh, how she wanted so badly to stay here forev—

"I'm afraid not," she said.

He looked crestfallen at her response, and she had to sit on her hands to keep herself from reaching out to him.

"I'll help where I can today," she offered, amazed to realize she actually didn't mind doing it. Maybe as long as there were two of them, she and Chance would be evenly matched with the children.

Oh, who was she kidding? The Mongol Horde wouldn't have been a match for Quinn and Finn Foley.

Chance brightened at her offer, his grin broadening. Poppy tried not to spontaneously combust.

"Really?" he asked with all the earnestness of a child being told he could keep the puppy that followed him home. "Thank you so much. It'll be so helpful. You know these kids, right? They know you."

She sighed. "They used to know me. Until this week, I hadn't seen them for years. The last time I saw them, they were still…" *Sweet*, she remembered. Funny. Curious. Honestly, they had been delightful when they were babies. Before their parents spoiled them.

"They were still small," she finally finished. "I'm not sure they even remember me that well."

"Why didn't Logan and Adele make you their guardian?" Chance asked. "Don't get me wrong," he hurried to clarify. "I'm perfectly willing to take on the job. But I never even knew my niece and nephew existed until this week. I can't help feeling like they must have had other people in their lives they would have been more comfortable going to live with. People like you, for instance."

"Adele did ask me once if I would be their guardian," Poppy confessed, "shortly after the children were born."

"Why didn't you take her up on it?"

Poppy thought back to that afternoon six years ago. She had been stunned by the request. Not just because Adele, at twenty-four, was already thinking about the possibility of her death, but because Poppy, at twenty-five, had just graduated from law school and was thinking about everything *but* the possibility of her death. All the work that lay ahead for her, all the powerful people she would meet, all the important cases she would try. There was no way she could make any plans for the future at that point. Especially plans that involved responsibility for other people. Other little people, at that.

"I was young," she told Chance, hoping that would be enough to cover the explanation. But when he only continued looking at her expectantly, she added, "I don't want to have children. It's not who I am. I wouldn't be a good mother."

He looked surprised. "How can you be so sure? I mean, I never planned to become a father, either, but not because I don't think I'd be good at it. At least I'm going to try."

"But that's just it," Poppy said. "Being a parent isn't something you can stop doing because you re-alize belatedly you're not good at it. You can't return a baby to the baby store and say, 'You know what?

I need to return this. I'm just not that good at parenting, so I'd like to exchange this for a saxophone. Maybe I'll have a better talent for music.' You can't do that. You have to keep being a parent."

Even though, Poppy knew, there were some situations, some parents, for which such an opportunity would be better than keeping a child they'd stopped wanting. Or never wanted in the first place. Or were constantly disappointed by. Like, for instance, her own parents.

"Oh, I bet you could do anything you put your mind to, Poppy Digby."

It was the first time he'd said her name, and somehow, he made her feel as if he'd been saying it to her for years. Affectionately, at that.

Oh, this was not good. This was very, very not good. She never should have offered to help him out today. She should have stuck to her intentions and gotten the hell out of Dodge while she still had the chance.

Poppy winced. She would *not* have Chance. Not the capitalized one, anyway.

"There's still a lot we need to go over," she told him, gesturing toward the pile of papers in front of her. "Adele and Logan's will, their real-estate holdings, the children's medical and educational records…"

"Can we do that this afternoon?" he asked. "I'm

suddenly really anxious to meet my niece and nephew."

Oh, if he was anxious now, just wait until the end of the day.

"That's fine," Poppy said. Lionel, she was sure, would be grateful to be liberated from his baby-sitting gig.

Chance rose. "Hopefully, the four of us spending the day together will make the transition easier for the kids."

Poppy hoped so, too, as she stood. And she wondered if it was too early in the day for a martini, just in case.

"I've done my best to make the house comfortable for them until their stuff arrives from Boston," he continued. "I figure they won't mind making do with sleeping bags until their furniture arrives, but if they'd rather, I have a hide-a-bed in my office they can use until then."

"The movers promised to have their things here by Thursday at the latest," she said.

"Guess it's a good thing I never got around to furnishing my spare bedroom, huh?" he said. "And I'll be done dismantling my home office, so the kids will each have their own space. It won't be any trouble to turn it into a bedroom, too. I can start using the office at the shop for everything.

I probably won't be doing much work from home anyway, anyway."

She started to tell him he didn't have to upend his life for the children, but she knew that wasn't true. Even in the best of situations, children upended everything. She just hoped the three of them could eventually create a life together that, if not perfect, would at least be reasonably free of challenges.

"And I stocked up on kid-friendly groceries," he added as the two of them exited into the hall. "I hope they're still kid-friendly, anyway. I loved Dino Buddies when I was a kid."

Please stop, Poppy wanted to tell him. Because with every word he spoke, he grew more endearing. And she simply could not afford to be endeared right now. She had a corporate ladder to climb, one she'd been clawing her way up with icy, ruthless, cutthroat intent for years, without a care for whom she stepped on along the way. Okay, well, maybe not quite clawing. And she hadn't actually stepped on anyone. Just sort of nudged them aside with an under-the-breath *Excuse me*. She had been icy, ruthless and cutthroat, though. She still was. She *was*. Ask anyone.

Anyway, she was so close to the top of that ladder at this point. So close. Once she won her upcoming case—it went without saying that she would win, because Poppy hadn't lost one yet—she would make full partnership in her firm. It was the thing she'd set her sights on for more than a decade. The most important thing in the world.

"Oh, and I checked my attic," Chance continued, "because I was pretty sure I still had all my old LEGO and Hot Wheels and Pokémon cards. I don't know if kids are still into that stuff, but at least it might be a distraction for them until I can get them squared away."

Oh, my god, could the man be any sweeter? Poppy wondered as they made their way to the room where she'd left Lionel and the children. Even a day with him was going to wreak havoc on her heart. Her icy, ruthless, cutthroat heart that no one—*Do you hear me, Chance Foley? No one!*—would ever be able to breach.

"Thanks again for helping out today," he told her as they crossed the lobby.

"It's the least I can do," she said.

Which actually wasn't true. The least she could do was warn him about the feral wolverines who were about to take over his life and give him a chance to change into some Kevlar. She paused in the middle of the lobby.

"There's something I should tell you about the children, Chance, before you actually meet them."

Belatedly, she noticed she'd used his first name. Belatedly, she discovered how natural, even enjoyable, it felt to do it. Belatedly, she realized she wanted to use it a lot more.

He stopped, too. "Is there a problem?"

She sighed, struggling to find the right words. "Adele and Logan were a little overwhelmed by their sudden wealth. Virtually overnight, they went from struggling to make rent on a one-bedroom apartment in a marginal neighborhood to owning outright a town house in an area that's been upscale for three hundred years. From public transportation to a Mercedes and a Ferrari. From store-brand frozen pizza to a personal chef. That kind of thing."

Chance nodded. "Yeah, I can see where Logan would go a little overboard once he came into that much money."

"They didn't just go overboard," Poppy told him. "They treated themselves to whatever their hearts desired, and they gave their children everything they wanted and never curbed their...shall we say, less-than-stellar behaviors? Without the discipline young children need to learn about personal responsibility and consideration for other people, Quinn and Finn have become something of a challenge."

"Logan and Adele spoiled them rotten, you mean," Chance said with a smile.

"I don't think they meant to," Poppy said.

"It doesn't help that they just lost their parents," Chance added.

"No," Poppy agreed. "It doesn't. It's hard to know what's going on inside their little heads, but I suspect their behavior has worsened since their parents' deaths."

"Thanks for that reminder," he said. "I've been so focused on making sure they have all the physical comforts of home that I haven't really thought about their emotional needs."

Some of that, Poppy thought, could also be due to the fact that Chance had lost his own parents when he was little more than a child himself. Her heart went out to all three of them.

"It's not going to be easy for any of you in the coming weeks," she said gently. "Quinn and Finn are smart and resourceful, and they're good at creating pandemonium in order to get attention. But they're not bad kids. In spite of their wealth, they've grown up a bit disadvantaged."

He nodded his understanding.

"Well, all right, then," she said as she strode toward the office where she'd left them in Lionel's care. "Let's go introduce you to your niece and nephew."

She pushed the door open and took a step inside, with Chance on her heels. Although she wouldn't have been surprised to find Lionel tied up in the corner with the children performing dark arts around him, she was surprised to see the three of them sitting around a long table, seemingly now at ease. Though she couldn't help noticing that a painting on the opposite wall—one of Picasso's weeping women portraits—was splattered with what doubtless had been the remnants of Finn's replacement pineapple matcha latte.

The children were engrossed in their respective phones, and Lionel, holding a tube of superglue in one hand, was putting the finishing touches on the repair of Ms. Novak's award. Truth be told, it actually looked kind of cooler with all those broken shards pieced back together. Like a mini disco ball that beautifully caught the sunlight streaming through the windows beyond. It couldn't have been easy putting that thing back together as well as he had. Especially while fielding a lobbed pineapple matcha latte.

"There," he said as he glued the last piece into place. He looked up at Poppy and Chance gratefully. "It's not perfect, but at least it's a sphere. Maybe Ms. Novak won't notice."

At the comment, Finn glanced up from his phone—or, rather, Lionel's phone—to see what was going on. Lionel looked up, too, and when he saw Finn gazing at him, he hugged the award close to his chest and warily rose. Unfortunately, when he took a step in retreat, clearly worried that Finn was going to try something funny, Lionel tripped over the leg of his chair and went down, flailing.

So did the crystal globe, which shattered all over again. Lionel swore like a sailor. Quinn and Finn repeated the newly discovered epithet in a shouted chorus. Six times.

From behind Poppy, Chance echoed the sentiment, but thankfully did it quietly enough that the children wouldn't hear.

She expelled a totally fake sound of cheerfulness. "Well. Let's just hope that Picasso is a reproduction. Otherwise, the children have just kissed a good chunk of their inheritance goodbye."

Chapter Three

Chance knew he had to tread lightly here if he didn't want this whole thing to go south before he even said hello to the kids. They were going to be a part of his life for, well, the rest of his life, so the sooner he set boundaries, the better. At least, that was what he'd learned in the handful of online articles he'd read about raising kids…before he got too panicky to read the rest of those articles.

Had he been asked a week ago what a typical six-year-old looked like, he would have envisioned… Actually, he wouldn't have been able to envision anything, since, until a few days ago, he'd never thought about kids at all and had certainly never given any consideration to having some of his own. Not just because he'd never been in a particularly serious relationship with anyone that might stir such thoughts, but because he'd been part of a family once, and it hadn't gone well. Call him an alarmist, but he wasn't all that keen to repeat the experience of having one again.

Now, however, he had no choice but to repeat it. Maybe the family he was about to create for these kids wouldn't be the same as the one he'd known before, but he would still have to create a family for these kids. With these kids. He was going to be, for all intents and purposes, their father. And they would be his children. The implication of that was honestly just now hitting him. Like a Mack truck. Going a hundred miles an hour. Filled with cement.

As Poppy hurried to help Lionel clean up the mess scattered around him, Chance studied the children. Finn and Quinn Foley were as close to being identical as fraternal twins could be, and both were mirror images of Logan with their dark auburn hair and even darker eyes. Chance and his brother hadn't shared many physical traits in common, each of them favoring a different parent. Finn and Quinn reminded Chance of his mom. A lot. With any luck, they had her disposition, too—however deeply hidden it might be at the moment—and they'd ultimately show themselves to be sunny and even-tempered once they worked through the current upheaval in their lives.

As if he'd spoken the thought out loud, both children glanced at him in tandem, sharing identical expressions of wariness and defiance.

"We're not calling you Dad," Finn said by way of a greeting.

He was missing a tooth in front, Chance noted, and had a small scratch across the bridge of his nose. A too-small Ninja Turtles Band-Aid covered a scabbed-over contusion on the knee he had bent in front of him on the chair, and his shin bore a small bruise. Typical childhood injuries, Chance couldn't help thinking. He'd had more than a few of those himself growing up, thanks to skateboards and bicycles and irresponsibly used Slip 'N Slides. Somehow, the abrasions were kind of comforting, as if Finn were just a normal kid, one whose whole world wasn't currently out of whack.

"That's fine," Chance told him. He forced a smile. "You can call me anything you want. Just don't call me late for dinner."

Dad jokes. That was another thing he was going to have to master. His own father had been the champion of them. The late-for-dinner one had been a favorite of his. Chance had thought it was hysterical when he was a kid. Finn seemed less impressed.

"Okay. I'm gonna call you Uncle Stupidhead."

As Chance tried to frame a reply to that, Quinn smiled at him, too. Like her brother, she was missing a tooth in front, albeit a different one, and her hair was cut short. She sat in her chair the same way Finn did in his, with one leg drawn up before her. Her sandaled foot revealed toenails painted in alternating bright turquoise and orange, though the polish was chipped on every one. The same polish was just as patchy on her fingernails, and those, Chance saw, were bitten down to the quick.

"Hi, Uncle Stupidhead," she said.

Hoo-kay. Not off to the best start with his new family. He probably shouldn't have told the kids they could call him anything they wanted. His dad humor definitely needed some tweaking. He did his best to backtrack good-naturedly. "Oh, come on. Why would you call me something like that?"

They looked at him as if he were an idiot. Which, okay, they'd already made clear they thought he was.

"Because you're our uncle," Finn said.

"And a stupidhead," Quinn added cheerfully.

"I am indeed your uncle," Chance agreed. "So you can for sure call me that. But what makes you think I'm a stupidhead? You just met me."

"We can just tell," the children replied as one.

Okay, grief-stricken children whose world had been upheaved or not, Chance wasn't going to give them a pass on their rudeness. It was probably best if he made clear right off the bat that he wasn't going to tolerate them bad-mouthing him or anyone else.

"Um, yeah, you can't call me Uncle Stupidhead," he told them levelly. "You can call me Uncle Chance. Or just Chance, if you'd rather. Sound good?"

In response, the children ignored him. He started to say something else, but by now, Poppy and Lionel had scooped up most of the mess, and the latter was leaving the room with Olympian speed, calling out something over his shoulder about putting together an invoice for the damage the children had caused.

Poppy watched him go with clear envy at his escape, then turned to Chance and brightened. Some. A little. Okay, the improvement in her mood was barely noticeable. Chance would take what he could get.

"On the upside," she said, "the Picasso is definitely a reproduction. He used a much richer red, and last time I checked, the original is in the Tate Gallery."

Clearly, famous economists and cacti weren't Poppy Digby's only areas of interest. It struck Chance then that the two of them couldn't be more different from each other, since his own interests—other than boating—included small-batch rye whiskeys and Things to Do with a Grill, and the only art he was familiar with were those Live, Laugh, Love plaques Ivy Clutterbuck sold at the Saturday farmers' market. So why was he so attracted to Poppy, so immediately, even in her disheveled state? Then again, maybe it was her disheveled state that had done it. As efficient as she clearly was, and as much as she obviously strove for perfection, she seemed unbothered by the fact that she was currently—there was no way to sugarcoat it—a train wreck.

"Don't take the *Uncle Stupidhead* to heart," she added softly enough so the children wouldn't hear. "It could be worse. They call me Poopy."

"And you let them?" Chance asked.

"Trust me, this is not the hill you want to die on. There are going to be more." She closed her eyes, inhaled a deep breath and released it slowly. "So many, many more."

Spoken like a woman with hair sticking up, stained clothing, smudged lipstick and weird green matcha stuff on her chin. Without thinking, he lifted his hand and, as gently as he could, traced his thumb over the offending splotch. Immediately, her eyes snapped open, and she jerked her head back, taking a step away from him. Her hand flew to the place he had just touched, and she looked stunned by what he had just done.

"I'm sorry," he said immediately.

He was kind of stunned by what he'd just done, too. He wasn't the type to get all handsy with a woman he'd just met. Hell, even some of his ex-girlfriends had complained he wasn't physically demonstrative enough. What was it about Poppy that had him acting in a way he'd never acted before? In a lot of ways he'd never acted before? He told himself everything was weird because he'd just been dropped into a weird situation. When he looked at her again, though... There was something there that went beyond weirdness. Something he'd honestly never felt before. And he was pretty sure it had nothing to do with the situation and everything to do with her. And him. And them.

"I'm sorry," he said again. "I just... I mean, you just..." He lifted his hand to point to the place on his own face where the stain of green still lingered on hers. "You have something on your chin. I was just trying to help get it off."

Her gaze never left his—and she never moved her hand from her face—as she backed toward the briefcase she'd dropped on the floor beside Lionel's recently vacated chair. She fumbled around in it until she located what she was looking for—a small hand mirror she held in front of her face. When she saw her reflection, her eyes widened in panic.

She withdrew a handkerchief from her pocket and began to scrub furiously at the green stain.

Then she scrubbed at her smudged lipstick. Then at the errant tufts of hair. All with mixed results.

Behind him, the children started giggling in a way that reminded Chance of a horror movie he'd seen when he was a teenager, one that had left him sleeping with the lights on for a month afterward. Nope. He was not going to turn around and look at the kids. Because number one, he was pretty sure they were only trying to get attention. And number two—just in case he was wrong about number one—he didn't want to see their heads spinning around on their shoulders while blood spewed out of their eye sockets. Been there, done that.

He started to ask Poppy if he could help, but she abruptly halted her efforts and stuffed both mirror and handkerchief back into her jacket pocket. "I need to get back to my hotel," she announced. "Checkout is at noon, and they pretty much threatened torches and pitchforks if I was even a minute late, because there's evidently some kind of event going on in town that has rooms here at a premium."

"Welcome Back Bob," Chance told her.

She looked confused. "I beg your pardon?"

He chuckled. "That's the event that's going on. The Welcome Back Bob Comet Festival. To celebrate the return of Comet Bob."

She nodded vaguely. "Right. That's the comet

I've been seeing in the headlines on my newsfeeds for the past couple of weeks."

"That's him."

"Him?" she echoed. "Comets have genders?"

"This one does. At least to the residents of Endicott."

"I didn't realize it was a big enough deal to warrant festivals. But then, I don't really read the science news much," she added. "I'm more of a *Bloomberg Business* and *Wall Street Journal* kind of gal."

"Yeah, well, I'm more *WoodenBoat* than *Scientific American* myself," Chance told her. "But here in Endicott, you pretty much have to be comet-obsessed by law. At least you do every fifteen years, when this one comes around."

When she still looked a little baffled, he had to remind himself that there was a whole wide world out there for whom Comet Bob was just another cool thing that showed up in the night sky every once in a while. But here in Endicott, even during the years when the festival wasn't going on, there were still vestiges of him all over the place, from street art to restaurant menu offerings to school mascots.

"I'm actually kind of surprised you were able to find a room last night," he told Poppy. "Usually all the local hotels are booked solid this time of year."

"I gather I got the last one, and it was only available for one night because today is apparently when people really start arriving in droves."

"Yeah, this is the big week when Bob makes his closest pass to the planet. He'll be directly overhead Thursday night. The closer he gets, the wilder things—and people—are going to get. Probably just as well you're getting out of town when you are."

Even though he really wished there were some way she could stay around for a few days more. Or until the kids were doing one of those gap years abroad.

"What do you mean?" she asked.

"I mean, there are a lot of legends surrounding the comet," he told her. "And some of them are probably going to get a little out of hand this week."

"What kind of legends?"

He lifted one shoulder and let it drop. "A lot of people think Bob creates cosmic disturbances that lead to all kinds of chaos and make people do things they'd normally never do. See stuff that isn't there. Swipe right when they'd normally swipe left. There's even the belief that Bob makes wishes come true. That kind of thing."

Poppy smiled. "You don't seem to be one of the people who thinks those things."

Despite the fact that his wish to Bob fifteen years ago was essentially coming true this year, Chance said, "Not really. I feel like a lot of it is just self-fulfilling prophecy stuff. People think Bob makes them act weird and do things they shouldn't, so they act weird and do things they shouldn't, and then they just blame it on Bob. Ordered a double cheese-burger instead of a garden salad? Oops. That's just Bob. Spent the money you've been saving up for a house on a sports car instead? Oh, no. It was be-cause of Bob. Caught having a fling with the pool man? Yeah, we're definitely gonna blame that one on Bob."

"Bob sounds pretty busy," Poppy said, grinning.

Chance grinned back. "Oh, he's just warming up."

A soft sound from behind them made them both turn around to look at the children. They seemed to be listening *very* closely to his exchange with Poppy. He hoped what he'd said about the pool man fling went over their heads and made yet another mental note to watch what he said in the future be-cause there were going to be children around. For the rest of his life.

"You can make wishes on a comet?" Quinn asked.

"And he makes them come true?" Finn added.

"Well, they only come true if you were born in Endicott during a year when the comet came around and then make the wish the next time he comes around," Chance told them. At the children's crestfallen expressions, he hurried to recapture their interest. "I mean, at least that's what people say. Who knows if you really have to be born in Endicott or in a year of the comet? Maybe Bob grants all the wishes people make whenever he comes around."

The children perked up again, exchanging excited looks. Then they looked back at Chance.

"When were you born?" Finn asked.

"I was born when the comet came around thirty years ago," he said, noting reluctantly that he sounded a lot like a proud believer in comet legends. He couldn't help it. It was nice to have the kids engaged in something in a normal childlike way.

"Did you make a wish when he came back again?" Quinn asked.

"I did," he said.

"Did your wish come true?"

There was really no good way to answer that. Technically, the million dollars he'd wished for fifteen years ago had become a reality on this visit from Bob, but it was conditional and wouldn't be arriving in his bank account for another fifteen or so years. And even at that, there was nothing to prove the comet was behind it. Although it would have been fun to think Bob had made his teenage wish come true, Chance was pragmatic enough to consider it more of a coincidence than anything else. Not to mention he didn't want to think about a wish coming true because someone had died. That was just too troubling to consider. So he was going to go with coincidental.

So he only told the kids, "I don't know yet."

"What did you wish for?"

Surprisingly, it wasn't one of the children who asked the question. It was Poppy. And she had kind of a dreamy look in her eye when she said it, as if she'd been almost as swept away by the conversation about comet magic as the children were.

Chance smiled. "I'm not telling."

A trio of disappointed sounds went up around him.

"Oh, come on, Uncle Chance!" Finn said.

"Yeah!" Quinn concurred.

"Nope," Chance insisted, ridiculously happy to be Uncle Chance instead of Uncle Stupidhead—at least for the time being. "It might not come true if I tell."

And, weirdly, even though it had pretty much come true, there was something that still felt missing from the wish, some part of it that was still out there lingering in the cosmos, as if Bob wasn't willing to completely reveal his hand yet.

Poppy seemed to snap out of her dreamy state and looked down at her watch. "I really do have to get going," she said. "The original plan was for Lionel to drive me to Louisville after I checked out of the hotel—I was going to do some sightseeing, then take a rideshare to the airport. But now that I'm staying in town all day, I'm not sure Lionel will be available."

"What time is your flight?" Chance asked.

"I need to be at the airport by six thirty. My flight leaves at eight twenty-five."

"Do you have any bags to check?"

She shook her head.

"You can get to the airport by seven thirty," he assured her. 'Cause, by god, he was going to squeeze every single minute out of her promised extra time that he could.

"But—"

"It's Louisville, not Boston. The lines aren't that long. An hour before your flight is fine, especially if you don't have any bags to check. Trust me."

"But—"

"I can drive you to the airport," he offered. "Well, I and the kids can. Right, kids?"

Their momentary enthusiasm over Comet Bob evaporated, and they looked none too thrilled to be driving Poppy to the airport. Granted, it would be more than an hour's drive round trip. On the other hand, being cooped up in a car that long would give him and the kids a chance to get to know each other better. Whether they liked it or not.

"No," Finn said with more conviction than a six-year-old should have.

Chance suddenly felt like a lowly peon being stared down by the company CEO. Which was doubly strange since he was his own boss. At least, he used to be. Before two six-year-olds entered the picture.

"Excuse me?" he replied automatically.

"No," the boy repeated even more emphatically. "We don't want to take Poopy to the airport with you."

"Yeah, Uncle Stupidhead," Quinn chimed in. "We wanna get pancakes for dinner."

Well, that was going to be a problem, because Chance was jonesing for Dino Buddies. Taking a page from Poppy's book where Lionel and his phone were concerned earlier—the page headed *Bribery*—he asked them, "Hey, have you guys ever had a Modjeska?"

The children narrowed their eyes curiously but said nothing.

"Come on," Chance cajoled. "Have you? I bet you haven't."

The children looked at each other, then back at Chance.

"What's a…?" Finn started to ask. He seemed to not want to tackle the last word.

"A Modjeska?" Chance supplied helpfully. "It's

awesome, that's what. And the only place you can get *real* Modjeskas is in Louisville." Yeah, okay, you could get them on Amazon, too, but that wasn't a big deal since you could probably get an ICBM on Amazon, if you looked hard enough. Anyway. "On our way back from taking Poppy to the airport tonight," he continued, "we can stop at Muth's Candies and I'll buy you a whole bag of Modjeskas."

The children looked curious. "What are they?" Quinn echoed.

Chance made what he hoped was a dad-like silly face. "They're awesome," he repeated in a similarly silly voice—he hoped. "Duh. I just told you that."

Finn and Quinn narrowed their eyes at him again, clearly not cool with having their own intelligence impugned. Score one for Uncle Stupidhead.

"But—" they started to say.

Wanting to hang on to the upper hand for as long as he could, Chance interrupted, "Hey, let's get Poppy back to her hotel, okay? Then we'll find something fun to do around town. There's a ton of stuff going on today. I'm sure we'll be able to find something to keep us busy."

Chance was as good as his word, Poppy discovered not long after they left the law office. Better, in fact, because he bore the brunt of the children's shenanigans like a champ, giving her an opportunity to catch her breath for the first time in a week. She'd even had time to change clothes before checking out of the hotel, a change that, for once, didn't include pounding on and screaming through the bathroom door, followed by the discovery of something broken in her apartment. Though, as fine as they were for airline travel, beige linen trousers and a white silk blouse—not to mention her great-aunt Theodora's pearls, which were a staple of her wardrobe—weren't the ideal garments to wear for a day she'd be spending with notorious food-hurlers. She was packed and out of her room by 11:58 a.m., and, even more miraculously, she didn't have to tell the hotel concierge to bill her for any damage. Quinn and Finn had simply been too exhausted from their travels last night to do anything but fall into bed.

She turned from the reception desk to see Chance and the children standing in the lobby. He was in much the same state she had been earlier, stained and bedraggled, his hair a fright, and looking as if he wanted to be anywhere but here.

"I thought it would be a good idea to get the kids some lunch at Bud's Build-a-Burger," he said by way of an explanation as she approached. "I was wrong."

She drew up to the trio cautiously, wheeling her carry-on behind her. "The concierge was just telling me there's a Fireball Fun Fair for kids at the park."

Even though, technically, comets weren't fireballs. She was beginning to realize this comet festival's activities weren't entirely rooted in actual scientific data. The people she'd seen on the drive back to her hotel who had been dressed up like cartoon neoprene planets and others covered head to toe in silver body paint had been a dead giveaway.

"Might be something the kids would enjoy," she added. And could potentially leave them as exhausted as an interstate flight had. It could happen.

"Something with rides?" he asked hopefully. "Rides that have seat belts and lots of centrifugal force that prevent things from moving?"

"Well, it wouldn't be much fun without centrifugal force, would it?"

"I'm down," Chance said. He looked at the kids. "How about you guys? Wanna go to the Fireball Fun Fair?"

"Will there be a real fireball?" Quinn asked in a way that Poppy found slightly concerning.

"Yes," she lied before Chance could tell them the truth. The promise of arson, she was sure, was guaranteed to convince the kids that a fun fair would be the perfect afternoon pastime.

Chance threw her a stern look in response. Poppy just smiled.

"Trust me." She echoed his earlier words.

He didn't look anywhere near convinced. Poppy

didn't care. She had only two things left on the day's to-do list: *keep the Foley children from destroying the world* and *make my flight back to Boston*. If she trusted Chance with the latter, then he could trust her with the former. For the first time in days, she felt like the Earth was settling back on its axis. If she could make it through the next six hours or so, everything was going to be just fine.

This time tomorrow, she would be back at her desk at Barrington, Toller & Riggs doing what she did best—putting together a defense for their client that would save them a literal fortune *and* set a precedent for anyone else who thought it was a good idea to accuse a multinational, billion-dollar corporation of being a bloated, arrogant, amoral villain. Never mind that her clients were, in fact, bloated, arrogant, amoral villains. It wasn't Poppy's job to judge the defendants in any of her cases. It was her job to uphold the law—regardless of how unpleasant that might be sometimes. The world of corporate law wasn't exactly overrun with rainbows, cupcakes and unicorns. But it was filled with money, influence and power. She was good at what she did, and she had her reasons for doing it. And this time tomorrow, she would be back at it again.

For today, though... Well, today hadn't exactly been filled with rainbows and unicorns, either. But there could be some cupcakes at some point. At least she could enjoy a few hours of not being focused on spreadsheets and annual reports and regulatory data. If she and Chance could keep the kids occupied, she might even have a little fun. And, hey, when was the last time she'd had a little fun?

She actually gave some thought to that. Surely, it hadn't been as long ago as the Associates Appreciation Brunch back in February. That had been kind of fun, though. In a still-have-to-wear-a-suit, what's-with-all-the-client-schmoozing, this-isn't-really-an-appreciation-brunch-is-it kind of way. And before that, last fall, she'd gone on that date. That one single, interminable date with Thomas from Intellectual Property. Who had been so fascinating when he talked about force majeure. For three hours. Yeah, that had been a blast.

"So…fireball?" she asked Chance and the kids.

Chance looked considerably less enthusiastic than the children. But he nodded. "Okay. Let's go find ourselves some centrifugal force. And funnel cakes. They usually have funnel cakes at fun fairs, don't they? Funnel cakes can fix anything."

Chapter Four

Okay, so maybe Chance had been wrong about the funnel cakes, he realized later, as the sun was beginning to dip toward the trees. Yeah, they could fix what had started off as a pretty anxious day, because the minute he tasted one, he was carried back to his childhood and some of the happiest moments of his life. And they could fix two children who were getting tired of seat belts and centrifugal force, because funnel cakes were covered with powdered sugar, which made it easy for said children to stick bits of said funnel cake to all kinds of things they really shouldn't have been sticking funnel cake to, like Mr. Garcia's blue-ribbon macaroni collage and Mrs. Cooperman's Dandie Dinmont Terrier, Eugene. They could even fix Poppy's raging headache that she got from downing a frozen lemonade way too fast, something for which he knew she had been eternally grateful. What they couldn't fix was the backed-up traffic on US Route 62.

He braved a glance over at Poppy, sitting in the passenger seat of his new Jeep Cherokee. She was looking at her watch, which she'd been doing pretty much nonstop ever since they turned onto 62…and immediately hit bumper-to-bumper traffic that was moving way too slow. Something that was super weird on a Sunday, even with the comet festival going on. They should have had a clear shot all the way to New Albany, then Louisville. Instead, they were stuck on the bridge over Blackbird Creek, not going anywhere and with no way to turn around.

"I'm going to miss my flight," Poppy said, not for the first time.

"It'll be fine," Chance assured her. Not for the first time.

"They're going to start boarding any minute now."

They probably were. Even so, he said, "I'm sure the traffic will clear once we're across the bridge. The interstate's not that far ahead, and then we'll make great time. It'll be close, but we'll make it."

Provided the traffic on the other side of the bridge wasn't at a standstill, too. Which it clearly was.

"And there are no other flights to Boston tonight," she told him.

"But you did PreCheck, right?" he asked, still focusing on the road ahead as if they were actually moving. "You're at Gate A1, which is right around the corner once you get through security. It's not that big of an airport. You'll be fine."

"If we start moving right now and keep moving," she said, pretty much reading his mind. She looked at the line of cars ahead of them, too. "We're not going anywhere. I'm going to miss my flight."

She was right. Unless his new car came with a rotor blade, stabilizer and rudder, which he was pretty sure hadn't been included in the dealer add-ons, they were stuck.

"How much longer till we get there?" Quinn asked.

It wasn't the first time for that comment, either.

"Soon," Chance told her. Though *soon* could mean *within the next forty-eight hours*. Or years. Or centuries.

"I'm hungry," Finn joined in. Which was impossible, since he'd brought a funnel cake with him and was still picking at it. "When do we get the majesties?"

"Modjeskas," Chance corrected him. "Soon," he promised again.

Though, in hindsight, promising the kids sugar on top of what turned out to be an afternoon filled with sugar hadn't been his finest moment. When it came to bribing children, sweets just understandably topped the list. However, sweets, he had learned the hard way today, were evidently jet fuel for anyone under the age of ten, and they should be rationed accordingly.

"I have to pee," Quinn said.

As should frozen lemonade.

He dipped his head to the steering wheel in defeat and sighed. "You're going to miss your flight," he told Poppy helplessly. "And I am so sorry. It's just so unusual for there to be traffic going into Louisville this time of day on a Sunday. There must be a wreck or something up ahead."

Poppy let out a sigh, too, though hers was more of the resigned variety than the angry kind, something that surprised Chance. She had every right to lay into him for making her miss her flight. He'd been cocky and overly optimistic, and she was the one who would be paying for it.

"It's fine," she said wearily. She pulled out her phone and began scrolling through her call list. "I'll just see if I can book another night at the hotel and fly home tomorrow."

"I can take you to the airport," Chance said.

"No, no," she objected with surprising courtesy. "I can have Lionel do it."

"Really, I don't—"

"It's fine."

"But—"

She moved the phone to her ear, effectively silencing anything else Chance might say. Not that he blamed her. He wouldn't trust himself to get him to the airport on time, either. Then he listened—and managed to inch the car forward a bit—as she tried to book another night at her hotel and was told there were no rooms available. Then he inched the car forward some more and watched surreptitiously as she checked her phone for other available rooms in the area...and found none. By then, they were nearing the end of the bridge and what Chance knew was a gravel turnaround on the other side—one that many cars were taking advantage of, since traffic in the opposite direction was nonexistent. Thankfully, it wasn't long before he was able to take advantage of it, too. Because Quinn's demands for a bathroom were becoming ferocious, and Finn's assurances that he was nearing death by starvation were becoming voracious, and Poppy, he was pretty sure, was starting to cry, and holy crap, it was only day one of fathering and he was already a massive failure.

How was he going to get through more than a decade of this until the children could be on their own? What if the children were never able to be on their own? Was his entire life now going to be dedicated to the feeding and bladder-vacating of two small noisy children? Would he never know a moment's peace again?

Once he had the car turned around, he raced down the highway and screeched into the first gas station he saw as if he were Vin Diesel. Quinn hopped out of the car with Poppy on her heels, and Chance followed with Finn at a more leisurely pace. Oh, wait, no, it was actually at a more accelerated pace, because Finn couldn't get to the snack aisle fast enough. As he stuffed the last of the funnel cake into his mouth, he began scooping up every bag of chips he could get his grubby hands on. Good god, did the kid ever stop eating? On the upside, at least he wasn't consuming more sugar. On the downside, fat, salt and grease weren't going to be much better.

"Hey, Finn," Chance said, "how about instead of loading up on chips, we stop for a real dinner at a real restaurant on the way home?" He didn't add that the restaurant he had in mind was Endicott's sole vegan restaurant, Kay's So Raw So Raw.

Finn looked at him as he had nearly every other time that day, as if Chance wasn't operating at full capacity. Then he looked down at his armloads of chips. "This is a real dinner," he said matter-of-factly.

"There's no way your parents let you eat six bags of chips for dinner."

"Yes, they did."

Right. Because, according to Poppy, Logan and his wife had never denied the children anything. Chance was just getting his first taste of why giving children whatever they wanted was a bad idea.

"Yeah, well, I think after all the fair food today, we need to think about something more nutritious." Putting aside for now the fact that he himself had been planning to ply the children with candy after dropping off Poppy, then serving them Dino Buddies for dinner, he added, "If you guys don't want to go to a restaurant, we can pick up something on the way back to town."

"But—"

"One bag," Chance compromised. "You can have one bag to tide you over. Whichever flavor you like best."

Finn looked like he wanted to argue but, amazingly, put back all but one bag of chips. Barbecue flavor, Chance couldn't help noticing. That had been Logan's favorite flavor, too.

A strange melancholy settled over him. Since seeing the kids that morning, he'd remembered a lot about his brother that had been banished to the very back of his brain for too long. The kids didn't resemble their dad just in their looks and their, ah, challenging disposition. At the fair, their favorite ride had been the Tilt-A-Whirl, which had been Logan's, too. They'd turned their noses up at tacos, saying they didn't like Mexican food. Logan hadn't, either. And when the ROTC band at the festival had broken into "Lazy Bones"—Hoagy Carmichael was an Indiana treasure, after all—the kids had sung along perfectly, saying their dad had sung the song to them when they were little. Not surprising, since their mom had sung Hoagy Carmichael songs to her sons all the time. But where Chance's favorite had always been "Ole Buttermilk Sky," Logan's had been "Lazy Bones."

Chance would have sworn by now that he couldn't possibly miss his brother. It had been far too long since Logan had been a part of his life. And even when Logan was around, when they were kids, they'd had normal sibling struggles that kept them from being too close. But the more time he spent with Logan's children, the more Chance felt the presence of his brother back in his life. And he was surprised to realize the depth of his feelings about that. He was surprised, too, at the conflicting feelings. As much as he didn't miss Logan, he really kind of missed Logan. And he wasn't sure what to do with that.

Poppy and Quinn joined them, and Chance made a similar snack concession for his niece, who chose a bag of cheese corn—another favorite of Logan's—for her own.

"You want anything?" he asked Poppy.

Even without her saying it, he knew what she was thinking. She wanted to be on a plane that was tooling down the tarmac before taking off for Boston. His guilt at making her miss her flight doubled.

Instead of replying verbally, she went to the next aisle over—the chocolate aisle—and chose a packet of peanut butter cups. Not the usual size that held two pieces, but the industrial size that contained six.

"This will do," she said.

Chance passed on food for himself, paid for everyone else's selections, then corralled them all back into the Jeep. Poppy immediately went to work on her candy, and the telltale sound of plastic ripping in the back seat let him know the children were doing likewise. As he pulled back onto the highway, it seemed ridiculous to bring up dinner again. Probably, he should just drive them all home, and they could forage for something later, if anyone got hungry. Judging by the kids' eating habits today, that would probably happen right around the time they pulled into the driveway.

As they made their way back toward Endicott, the silence in the car was deafening. He turned on the radio, but a news report about the stagnant traffic on Route 62 made him turn it off again. So he anxiously fiddled with the rearview mirror, checked the side mirror, too, just to be sure, and marveled at the debacle his life was fast becoming.

"I'm sorry about your flight," he told Poppy again.

She fished another peanut butter cup out of its wrapper, stuffed it into her mouth whole and said nothing.

"And I'm sorry about your hotel, too," he added.

She chewed her candy in silence, stuck her hand into the wrapper for another, discovered to her dismay that it was empty and looked at Chance. "It's fine," she lied. "I don't mind sleeping on the street tonight. It'll be like camping. Except instead of a sleeping bag, I can cover up with the souvenir Welcome Back, Bob beach towel you won for me at the Shoot the Moon basketball throw."

"Don't be silly," he said. "You can stay at my place." When she looked as if she was going to object, he hurriedly added, "You can sleep in my room. I'll take the couch. It's not a problem. And I mean, what other choice do you have?"

She still looked as if she wanted to object, but she was a smart woman. She knew that Bob beach towel was way too thin to keep her warm, even on a balmy night.

"All right," she said softly. Then, almost grudgingly, she added, "Thank you. I appreciate it."

"Jeez, it's the least I can do."

"I'll book another flight when we get to your place. It'll be fine."

He hoped she was right. Not about booking another flight—there were plenty leaving Louisville every day—but that things would be fine. Because at the moment, Chance couldn't quite shake the feeling that *fine* was a word that wouldn't be wandering into his vocabulary very much in the future. In fact, he was beginning to wonder if things in his life would ever be *fine* again.

Poppy didn't think she'd ever been more exhausted in her life than she was as she stood in the shower in Chance's bathroom. Honestly, she could fall asleep right here, with hot water sluicing over her, and sleep for the rest of the week. After a late dinner of dinosaur-shaped chicken nuggets and something potatoey fashioned into smiley faces, she and Chance had gotten the children as settled in their new home as well as they could for now. The clothes they'd brought with them were stashed in a laundry hamper in the as yet unfurnished spare bedroom—soon it would become Quinn's bedroom—and two sleeping bags were unrolled on the floor, each topped by a pillow encased in cartoon characters about whose identities Poppy had no clue. Both sleeping bags were still empty at the moment, despite the fact that it was nearly midnight, because the children had insisted they couldn't go to bed until they'd thoroughly explored their new home.

Poppy gave her hair one final rinse and switched off the water. As she toweled herself off and donned a pair of striped pajama pants and a black T-shirt with a Ruth Bader Ginsburg quote, she found herself wondering if the children's need to explore had nothing to do with wanting to familiarize themselves with their new surroundings and everything to do with stalling. If she were in their situation, she probably wouldn't want to go to bed, either. It couldn't be much fun, facing the prospect of waking up tomorrow in a world they didn't recognize.

She combed her hair, zipped up her cosmetic bag and exited the bathroom into Chance's bedroom. His house, a two-story bungalow, was as charming as the rest of Endicott, all hardwood floors and natural wood trim and walls the color of café au lait. It was still clearly a work in progress, but the rooms he had finished were surprisingly homey with their patterned area rugs and vintage travel posters. He didn't have much in the way of personal touches like photographs and memorabilia, but considering the way he'd spoken of his sparse life before his mother's death, that wasn't particularly surprising.

What few personal mementos he did have were all in his bedroom, and Poppy felt oddly out of place among them. She didn't consider herself to be ultra-feminine, but seeing her aubergine suitcase open on his midnight blue club chair, spilling its contents of tailored blouse and skirt, seemed somehow impossibly girlie. The furniture in the room was all unfashionably large and sturdily carved, something that made her belongings seem even daintier. The walls were dotted with pictures of gorgeous wooden boats, two bookcases were stuffed with paperback mysteries and oversize copies of nautical lore, and the top of his dresser was cluttered with the flotsam and jetsam of his everyday life—wallet, keys, sticky-note reminders and two framed photographs.

It was toward those last that she was drawn after returning her toiletries to her suitcase. The first was fairly recent and depicted Chance and two other men—both as impossibly handsome as he was, she couldn't help noticing—seated on a sunny pebble-stone beach somewhere. Each was lifting a beer and smiling the sort of smile people did when they'd just enjoyed the best day ever. It was the second photo, however, that captured Poppy's attention more. It was of three boys who couldn't be more than ten posing at the foot of someone's suburban driveway.

They were wearing helmets of varying snazziness and were draped over identical BMX bikes. Clearly, the subjects of the two photos were the same guys spanned across decades. Poppy couldn't imagine what it must be like to have friends in your life for that long. Nice, probably. Very, very nice.

"It was the day after Christmas," Chance said from behind her, startling her.

She spun around to find him leaning in the doorway of his bedroom, and she suddenly felt guilty for some reason. She told herself her heart was only racing because he'd surprised her. Then she realized her pulse had been accelerated long before he spoke. It had started, in fact, the moment she entered his bedroom.

She looked at the photo again. All three boys were dressed for summer. Certainly, she didn't know a lot about the weather in Indiana, but she'd bet good money it got pretty cold in the winter.

"But you're all wearing shorts and T-shirts," she said.

He strode cautiously into the room, as if he weren't quite sure of his reception, even though this was his sanctuary. But he paused a good two feet away from her.

"Yeah, it was like twenty degrees that day," he said. "We didn't care. We all wanted the same thing for Christmas that year—the Mongoose XTRM—

and we all got it. Sweetest ride ever. So me and Max and Felix were gonna ride that day, temperature be damned."

Poppy replaced the photo next to its newer companion. "Where was this one taken?"

"That was a couple years ago in Cuba. We went down to visit Felix's extended family after his grandmother's death and spent a day surfing in Yumuri. Well, Felix surfed," he amended with a smile. "Max and I just did a lot of falling into the water. It was a great day, though."

"You three have been friends for a long time," she said.

He rubbed the back of his neck in a way that looked at once anxious and relaxed. "Max and I since birth—our moms taught at the same school. And we met Felix in preschool. So, yeah. It's been a while."

"Wow."

They stood for a moment in awkward silence, neither seeming to know what to say. Finally, Chance jutted a thumb over his shoulder toward the bed, and for one bizarre—and not particularly unpleasant—instant, Poppy actually thought he was going to suggest the two of them retreat to it.

Instead, he told her, "I put fresh sheets on the bed while you were in the shower. Sorry, they're flannel. I only have two sets, one for summer and one for winter. I hope you don't get too hot tonight."

Oh, she wasn't going to touch that comment with a ten-foot reply. "I'm actually a pretty cool sleeper," she sidestepped. "So they'll feel good."

There was another pregnant pause in the conversation when neither Poppy nor Chance seemed to know where to go next. He took another step toward her and stopped, smiling.

"What?" she said.

"Nothing," he replied. "You just... You smell like me."

"I had to use your shampoo and bodywash," she said apologetically. "I don't pack that stuff when I travel. I make do with whatever the hotel has. I'm sorry."

"No apology necessary," he assured her. "I kinda like it that you smell like me."

Normally, that kind of proprietary comment made Poppy want to poke a guy in the eye. But she didn't want to poke Chance in the eye. Because from him, the comment didn't sound proprietary at all. From him, it sounded...sweet.

He jutted his thumb over his shoulder again, this time toward the hallway behind him.

"I finally got the kids to take a bath. Finn's in the tub downstairs, and Quinn is up here, in the bathroom down the hall. I told them both to brush their teeth afterward. Any chance they'll listen to me?"

"Not likely," Poppy told him honestly.

"Yeah, I didn't think so. Guess we'll have to hover. But then hopefully after that, we should be able to get them into bed."

Much to Poppy's amazement, she and Chance were indeed able to get the kids into bed after their baths. Both were so tired, they brushed their teeth without incident and trundled off to their waiting sleeping bags, climbing in without hesitation. Although Chance had assured them they would each have their own room in their new home, they insisted on sleeping in the same room until their things arrived. As she tucked them in, Poppy thought again about how daunting it must be for the two of them to be entering into an entirely new life, literally overnight. They were so young, and they'd lost so much. But kids were resilient, right? They sprang back quickly, didn't they? And, all things considered, Chance was doing surprisingly well with them so far. Surely, it wouldn't be long before they felt more at home here.

As Chance lingered in the doorway, Poppy stretched out on the floor to lie on her stomach between the two children as she said her good-nights. "So my flight home tomorrow leaves at lunchtime," she told them, "which means we get to have a great fun breakfast together before Lionel comes to pick me up." She forced a smile she was nowhere close to feeling. "Uncle Chance said he's going to make pancakes for us. How about that?"

"But, Poppy, can't you stay for a little while longer?" Quinn asked softly, her voice tinged with something that sounded very much like fear.

Finn chimed in, "Yeah, Poppy, don't go back to Boston yet. Please?"

The fact that the children were suddenly calling her Poppy instead of Poopy—never mind using the word *please*—told her just how distressed they were that she would be leaving the next day. She was their last link to the only home they'd ever known, and soon she would be gone, and then they'd be well and truly trapped in a world that held nothing familiar. That had to be scary.

"I have to go home, sweetie," she said. "Remember how I told you I have a big case coming up soon? I mean, it's really, really important."

"But that's a whole week away," Finn said. "You could stay for a little while longer."

"I still have a lot of preparing to do," she tried to explain. "There are a lot of people I have to talk to, and a lot of reading I have to do, and lots and lots and *lots* of figuring out what I'm going to say in court."

"You can read here," Quinn said.

"And you can talk to people on the phone," Finn told her.

"And you can practice what you want to say on us," Quinn concluded happily.

Technically, they were right. As long as Poppy had her tablet and her phone, she essentially had access to everything she needed to finish putting together her case. Her paralegals were amazing, and, all modesty aside, so was she. But she didn't like the unknown any more than the children did. She wanted to be on her own turf when she prepared for battle. Boston was a powerful, energetic city, and it was impossible not to feel powerful and energized herself when she was there. Endicott, on the other hand, was cozy and serene, which were the last things she should be feeling when she was about to defend titans of industry with the ferocity and tenacity of a legal pit bull.

"I really need to be in Boston," she said again. But even she could hear a ripple of capitulation in her voice.

"But if you stay," Quinn said, "you can be here when our furniture gets here and help me arrange my room. How am I gonna know where to put my bed and stuff?"

"I'm sure your uncle Chance will be happy to help you with that," Poppy told her.

But, again, she felt her conviction slipping. She

told herself it was because Quinn had simply mastered the sad puppy eyes.

Finn added, "You're the only one who knows how to order that latte thing I like."

This was news to Poppy. Her lack of knowledge about his beverage preferences was what had landed many a drink on her wardrobe.

"You have to teach Chance how to order it," he continued. "That could take all week."

Oh, great. Now Finn was doing the puppy eyes, too. And he was even better at it than Quinn was.

"I'll write it down for him," Poppy promised.

Before they could chip away more of her determination, she gave each of them a quick kiss on the forehead, told them she'd see them in the morning and rose to make her way out the door. But with every step she took, something hard and unpleasant pricked at her heart. Her icy, ruthless, cutthroat heart suddenly seemed a lot less icy, a lot less ruthless and a lot less cutthroat. Damn those puppy eyes, anyway.

Don't look back, she told herself. The kids were just exhausted and feeling vulnerable at the moment. And so was she. In the morning, they were all going to be fine. Just…

Don't look back, she told herself again. *Don't look back, don't look back. Don't…look…back.*

Chance threw her a supportive look as she neared

the doorway, and she could tell he knew exactly what she was thinking. She switched off the overhead light when she reached the door—*You're almost safe! Don't look back!*—leaving the room bathed in the radiating illumination of the nightlight.

"Poppy?"

It was Quinn. And her voice slicing through the darkness, so quiet and tiny and helpless, sank a cold stone to the pit of Poppy's stomach.

"Poppy, please don't go," she said. Worse, her words were punctuated by a soft sniffle, something that made Poppy want to cry, too.

"Stay a little longer," Finn added. "Please?" He was sniffling, too.

All the chaos of the past week with the children was completely stripped from her memory at the sound of those two little voices. Poppy looked at Chance, silently pleading with him. But all he had to offer her was a sympathetic shrug. He would be no help at all.

Don't turn around, she told herself. But she knew it was too late.

With a heartfelt sigh, she spun around to look at the children. "All right," she said. "I'll stay until the rest of your things arrive, so I can help you guys get settled in once and for all. As long as it's okay with your uncle Chance."

"Are you kidding?" he replied immediately. "Stay all week if you want. Stay a month. Stay forever."

He chuckled, but she could tell he was only half joking. Even so, something in the sound made her feel better about what she was doing. No, not just better. For the first time in a long time, Poppy felt good. The kind of good she hadn't felt since…since never.

Before she could ponder the significance of that, the children were out of their sleeping bags and rushing toward her. They hit her with a double hug so hard she went tumbling back into Chance. Automatically, he opened his arms to catch all three of them, enveloping them in an embrace that was another new experience for her: the group hug. The Boston Digbys weren't a particularly demonstrative bunch when it came to displays of affection. The Endicott Foleys, however, were another matter.

Just as Poppy started to enjoy the hug—and she was surprised at how much she did enjoy it— Chance suddenly pulled back. Even when the children struggled to keep him included, he managed to disengage himself from the embrace, leaving the two of them clinging to her alone. He threw her what he probably meant to be a reassuring smile as he took a few steps away, but there was something about it that looked a little panicked, too.

Before she could say a word, however—not that she had any idea what to say—he clapped his hands together and announced, "Okay, bedtime. Tomorrow, pancakes for breakfast. Then we'll figure out something fun to do. Good night to all. See you in the morning."

And then, without another word, he was escaping—that was the only word Poppy could think of to describe it—out of the bedroom and down the stairs.

Chapter Five

Chance didn't slow down until he'd made it through the living and dining rooms, into the kitchen—where he stopped long enough to pour a couple of fingers of his favorite rye—and out the back door to the patio. Even then, he couldn't quite stop moving, pacing back and forth in an effort to burn off the sudden bolt of…whatever it was surging through his system.

He still wasn't sure why he had reacted to the children's hug the way he had. He only knew that, one minute, he'd been unbelievably relieved that Poppy was offering to stay in town for a few more days. And then he'd been amazed—and kind of delighted, truth be told—that the children were seeming to show genuine affection for him when they threw themselves at him and Poppy. But then...

But then. That was where things got weird. The embrace of a small body was...odd. Chance couldn't remember ever hugging or being hugged by a child. Quinn and Finn were just so small. When they'd encircled his waist with their little arms, and when he'd realized just how delicate, defenseless and, well, *small* they were, and how he was going to have to be their protector and paladin, keeping them safe from all the myriad and infinite dangers lurking out in the big wide world, and that he had a *family* now to take care of—

He felt panic welling in the pit of his stomach again. He stopped pacing, enjoyed a long generous slug of his drink and closed his eyes. He'd had a family once. And little by little, piece by piece, it had all been taken away from him. He'd barely been more than a child himself when Logan, the last family member he knew, took off. Chance wasn't sure what to do with a family now. Other than risk losing it all over again.

"Are you okay?"

Poppy's voice from behind him was filled with concern. He turned to see her standing in the back door, looking more like a normal person than the starched and pressed attorney she'd been that morning. She'd stashed the pearls, and in place of her sensible heels, she was wearing little black slippers. Her hair was still damp from her shower, her tortoiseshell glasses were gone and her pajama choice was… interesting. Instead of answering her question, he gestured toward her shirt.

"When there are nine what?" he asked.

She glanced down at her T-shirt, then back at Chance. She still looked concerned, and he could tell she wasn't going to let him get away without answering her question at some point. But she seemed okay with letting it slide for now. She strode through the back door, leaving it open behind her, and crossed to the middle of the patio, where he stood. In spite of it being September, southern Indiana was still enjoying the occasional warm summer night. So it couldn't have been a chill in the air that made her cross her arms over her midsection. Something did, though.

She said softly, "When Ruth Bader Ginsburg was asked when she thought there would be enough women on the Supreme Court, she famously replied, 'When there are nine.' And when people were surprised by her answer, she pointed out that no one ever had a problem with there being only nine men." She lifted her shoulders and let them drop. "She's my hero for a lot of reasons. That's just one of them."

Chance nodded. "So are you gonna wind up on the Supreme Court someday, too?"

She laughed lightly. "No. I harbor no such aspirations nor delusions." She took a few more steps into the night, moving past Chance to the edge of the patio, her arms still hugging her torso. "Just don't tell my parents that," she added as she stared up at the sky.

"Why shouldn't I tell your parents that?"

She continued to gaze up at the stars. Chance's backyard abutted a nature preserve claiming a couple hundred acres, and his neighbors on both sides were a good fifty feet away. And because they were so removed from town, no one ever bothered to turn on any outdoor lights. On clear nights like this one, thousands of stars—and sometimes even the Milky Way itself—were visible in the night sky.

"Because they won't be satisfied until that's exactly where I am," she said. Her voice was edged with something he couldn't quite identify, but he got the feeling she was no more contented at the moment than he was. "Though even sitting on the Supreme Court probably wouldn't be enough for them to be satisfied with me, either. The sky is beautiful here," she hurried on in a lighter tone. Well, a little lighter. "I'm lucky if I see one star at night where I live in Boston."

He knew she was trying to change the subject.

But he didn't want her to. They'd shared one hell of a day today. They'd be sharing more days before she left. And they'd be sharing two kids for the foreseeable future. Maybe they wouldn't be running into each other on a daily basis, but they'd be in touch from time to time. He wanted to get to know Poppy Digby better. And not, he made himself admit, just because of the kids.

He covered the handful of steps between them until he was standing beside her, looking at the sky, too. She was right. It was beautiful. He couldn't remember the last time he'd noticed that.

"Is Ruth Bader Ginsburg the reason you decided to study law?" he asked.

For a moment, she continued to gaze at the stars, and he didn't think she was going to answer. "No," she finally said. "That was decided for me long before I was born."

She didn't elaborate, so Chance asked, "How did that happen?"

She expelled a restless sound and gave him a look that said, *You're not going to leave this alone, are you?* Which, of course, he wasn't, so he only sipped his drink and smiled.

"My parents are both outrageously successful attorneys," she told him. "My older brother and older sister are outrageously successful attorneys. My grandfather and grandmother Digby are retired outrageously successful attorneys. My great-grandfather Digby and great-great-grandfather Digby were outrageously successful attorneys. All of the Boston Digbys, for six generations, have been outrageously successful attorneys." She hesitated. "Well, except for my great-aunt Theodora Digby, who made rather a name for herself in burlesque under the name Titter O'Biscuit. But no one in the family is allowed to speak her name. Neither of them."

Chance laughed. "Okay, you just made that up."

"I did not," she assured him. She smiled, and it was genuine, and he was strangely happy to have cheered her up. "Although she died before I was born, Great-Aunt Theodora is another one of my heroes, because she thumbed her nose at obligation and convention and did her own thing. The pearls I always wear? They belonged to Aunt Theodora. No one else in the family would touch them. But they're my most cherished possession."

"You didn't want to become a lawyer?" Chance asked.

She expelled another restless sound. "It's not that I didn't want to go into law," she said.

"Then what is it?"

"It's that I never had the opportunity to think about doing anything else."

"But you're a good lawyer, right?" he asked.

"Oh, I'm an *excellent* lawyer," she said confidently. "As icy and ruthless and cutthroat as they come."

"You couldn't be excellent if you didn't have at least some passion for what you do," he told her.

Her expression changed at that, but she said nothing.

"So what exactly do you do?" he asked. "You said you practice corporate law this morning, but that's a pretty broad field, isn't it?"

She looked up at the sky again. And again, she hesitated before she replied. Finally, quietly, she said, "I specialize in antitrust law."

Her reply surprised him. Not because he couldn't see her practicing that—he totally could—but because it seemed like an unusual specialty. "So you keep big monopolies from happening and give small businesses like mine more opportunities?" he asked. It was an admirable pursuit.

She winced a little, a gesture that found its way into her voice when she replied, "Kind of? Except I actually do exactly the opposite?"

Once again, he was surprised by her response. "You defend big monopolies and allow them to happen?" he asked, certain he must have misunderstood.

"What I actually do is help create them and allow them to get even bigger."

Chance couldn't quite keep himself from glaring

at her. "Which is the worst thing that can happen to small businesses like mine," he said. Now there was an edge in his voice, too.

"That's a matter of opinion," she replied. But even she sounded like she knew that was a load of hooey.

All he could manage in response was "Wow."

She looked at him again, apologetically this time. "I know what I do for a living makes me sound like the bad guy," she said, "but I'm the opposite of that, too, Chance. Laws are a thing, and they need to be upheld. I'm one of the people who makes sure they are."

"But your clients aren't exactly widows and orphans, are they?" he said. "They're massively powerful corporations who are trying to become more massive and more powerful so they can take over the world."

"Look, I don't disagree with you that corporate America has a lot more power than it should. But don't blame the lawyers for that. Blame the laws. Until they're changed, it's my job to ensure that they're followed. And I'm very, very good at that. Because I've worked very, very hard. I want to make full partnership in my firm. And the case I have coming up is going to cement that for me when I win it."

"And that's important to you. A full partnership."

She looked genuinely surprised. "Of course it's important to me. It's the most important thing in the world to me. It's taken me years to get this far. I've sacrificed a lot. I've worked my butt off. Once I make partner, all of that will mean something."

"So just doing a good job isn't enough?"

Now she looked puzzled. "What do you mean?"

"Don't you find satisfaction in just knowing you've done your job well?"

"Do you?"

Chance shrugged. "Sure."

"I mean, I do, too," she backpedaled. "But I'd still like some recognition for my work. Is that so terrible?"

"No. I just don't think it should be the main reason for your work."

"It's not," she assured him.

Somehow, Chance knew that was true. But for some reason, he also got the impression that making partnership wasn't quite the main reason for all her hard work, either. Maybe there was more pressure from her family than she was willing to admit. Or maybe it was something else that only she understood.

"Anyway," she said, looking up at the sky once more, "in a few weeks, I'll be named partner, and then..." Her voice trailed off.

"And then what?" Chance asked.

"And then…" She sighed. "Can we talk about something else?"

But he was more interested than ever in learning more about her. Because the more he learned, the bigger the bundle of contradictions she became. Even so, he said, "Sure."

He gestured toward the three Adirondack chairs surrounding the firepit that he and Max and Felix generally occupied when his friends came over to grill. Naturally, Poppy gravitated toward the one Chance usually sat in himself. 'Cause that was what she did for a living—take things away from the small businessman.

Stop it, he told himself. Like she said, she had a job to do, the same as everyone else. Even if there was no way he could make the woman with wet hair wearing pajamas correspond to an icy, ruthless corporate cutthroat.

"You want something to drink?" he asked, belatedly becoming a good host.

She tucked her legs under herself in his chair and threw him a grateful smile. "I'd love a glass of wine if you have any."

He wasn't much of a wine drinker, but Felix always brought a bottle or two whenever he came over, so Chance had a few unopened ones lying around. And Felix, who had taken over the running of his grandmother's restaurant after her death and turned it into a regional epicurean hotspot, knew wine. So whatever was on hand had to be good.

"Red or white?" he asked Poppy.

"Red?" she said hopefully.

He nodded. He wouldn't mind topping off his own drink, anyway. It really had been one hell of a day. "I'll be right back," he told her.

Poppy watched Chance go inside the house and expelled a ragged sigh of relief. The last thing she wanted to do was offend him. But it was hard for her to defend to a small businessman like him why she did what she did for a living. Not just because it was hard for him to sympathize, but because there were times when she wasn't sure she understood it herself. She only knew that she was as driven as the rest of the Digby family was, that she was close enough now to taste such an achievement, and that it would be sweeter than anything she could imagine once she had it cinched.

She hadn't been lying when she told him she'd had little choice in her career. Her life had been planned out for her from the time she was a zygote in her mother's womb. Just like her parents and siblings and all the Digbys before them, she'd gone to the best schools and been one of the highest achievers in her class every year. Just like them, she'd attended Harvard Law and excelled in her chosen specialty. Just like them, she'd landed at one of the best law firms in Boston, and she'd proceeded to climb to the top. In fact, she would be the youngest Digby to make partner in his or her respective firm.

That was what happened when you were the youngest child of two super wealthy, super successful Beacon Hill attorneys who actually *were* icy, ruthless and cutthroat. To the point that they'd spent the bulk of their lives being icy, ruthless, cutthroat attorneys and the rest of their time holding Poppy and her siblings to an academic and social standard that no child should ever have to attempt, let alone perfect.

But all that Digby high achievement was fine with Poppy—it *was*—because she was a high achiever, too. It was only natural that she'd always been the best at whatever she did, from winning the spelling bees every year in grammar school to captaining the debate and lacrosse teams in high school, and then being number one in her undergraduate class at Boston University.

So what if she never won spelling bees at the national level when she was a kid? So what if the debate and lacrosse teams never had an undefeated season under her leadership? So what if she was number three in her class at law school? Once she made partner, she'd show her parents that she, too, had what it took to build a successful life like theirs.

This in spite of them constantly telling her while she was growing up that she just wasn't trying/working/struggling/fighting/wishing hard enough, and continuing to tell her that to this day. She'd heard it over and over—how it was just such a shame because she had *so much* potential she was throwing away. And why couldn't she be more like her brother and sister?

To hear her parents tell it, her life was such a waste.

She looked up to see Chance returning with her wine, and wow, not a moment too soon. He'd cleaned up, too, since they'd arrived home earlier and now looked adorably rumpled in a pair of baggy khaki shorts and a loose-fitting striped camp shirt, his feet encased in hiking sandals that had seen better days. His attire was a far cry from the crisp tailored suits and pointy-toed Italian shoes Poppy's male colleagues usually wore. Somehow, though, he looked way more appealing in his apparel than they did in theirs.

"I hope you like pinot noir," he said as he handed her a juice glass filled nearly to the brim with the stuff.

She smiled at the presentation. She wasn't sure if he just didn't know how to pour wine or if he'd somehow made himself privy to her thinking just now and knew instinctively what she needed.

"I love pinot noir," she told him as she accepted the glass gratefully.

She took an experimental sip and discovered it was delicious. Her surprise must have shown on her face, because Chance grinned.

"Yeah, I know," he said. "I'm not much of a connoisseur myself, but my friend Felix—the surfer in the photo upstairs? The one who didn't fall off and actually knows how to surf?—brought it over, and he owns a James Beard Award–winning restaurant here. So it should be pretty good."

He might as well have just told Poppy he was best friends with Gordon Ramsay. "A restaurant in Endicott has won a James Beard Award?" she asked dubiously.

"Two, actually," Chance said. "One for the restaurant and one for Felix himself. And he has a few more nominations from other years."

"We're eating there while I'm in town," she stated adamantly.

"Trust me. I think there's no way Felix will let us get away with *not* eating there while you're in town." He smiled cryptically at that, and although Poppy wanted very much to ask him about it, something told her she'd be better off not to.

He really was impossibly handsome. And charming. And sweet. Damn him. She simply could not afford to get distracted by handsome, charming, sweet men right now. Or ever, truth be told. Icy, ruthless, cutthroat attorneys like her weren't made or meant for romantic relationships.

Not that she wanted a romantic relationship with Chance. Or anyone. But especially Chance. All she wanted right now was to get through the next few days with him and the children and then go home to Boston. Home to her apartment—one that, even having lived there for years, she hadn't had time to arrange in any way that felt personal—where she could relax. As much as one could relax in an impersonal place. For a couple of hours every night before she had to turn in and get up to go to work the next day. Often for twelve or fourteen hours. Another reason she couldn't get involved with anyone. She couldn't even have a pet.

"So tell me about your small business," she said in an effort to change the subject to one where she wasn't thinking about how much she didn't want and couldn't afford a relationship with Chance. Realizing belatedly that she'd just ensured the spotlight would be firmly on him for a while. "You repair boats, yes?"

He nodded and took a seat in the Adirondack chair next to hers. "Among other things. I also build boats."

"Oh, I didn't realize you're also a boatwright. That's pretty impressive."

He looked surprised. "You know what a boat-wright is? That's pretty impressive, too."

"You can't grow up in New England without knowing what a boatwright is." Well, she supposed you could if you didn't grow up in the yachting community, as she had, but she didn't see any reason to go into specifics like that.

"I guess so. Anyway, boat building is really my passion," he told her. "My dad was a carpenter and taught me the trade when I was a kid. He mostly built houses and furniture, but because I liked spending time on the water so much, I gravitated toward boats. Unfortunately, it's hard to make a living building them. So I have the marine shop, too."

"Were you and your father close?"

He nodded. "Yeah, we were. Hurt a lot to lose him."

"How old were you when he died?"

"Twelve."

"Tough age to lose someone, but especially a father."

Chance sipped his drink thoughtfully and stared at something Poppy was sure she wouldn't be able to see, something that had nothing to do with the night and everything to do with his memories. Finally, he asked, "Are you close to your folks?"

She was surprised to realize she'd never been asked that question before. Which could be the reason why she had no idea how to answer it. She sipped her wine again, giving it some thought. Then, automatically, she told him, "As close as can be expected."

When he looked puzzled by the response, she had to admit that even she wasn't sure what she meant by it.

"I mean," she tried to clarify, taking another sip of her wine—it really was good, "they've always wanted what's best for me." Provided the best was what they had achieved themselves. "And they've always been my cheerleaders," she continued with another sip. As long as she was at the top of her game—woe betide her when she wasn't. "And they made a lot of sacrifices for me." Sip, sip, sip. Like that time they sacrificed their trip to New York to see *Hamilton* on Broadway because they were sure she needed extra grilling the night before her bar exam. And then never let her forget she made them miss the play that had been nearly impossible to get tickets for in the first place. "So…yeah," she lied. "I guess I'm pretty close to my parents."

When she lifted her glass to her mouth again, she was startled to discover it was empty. How had that happened?

"You want a refill?" Chance asked.

Oh, she definitely wanted a refill. In fact, he should probably just go ahead and bring out the bottle. "No, thank you," she said instead. "I'm beginning to feel the effects. Of the wine and the day. I should probably go ahead and turn in."

He nodded his understanding, then tipped the last of his own drink into his mouth. "Yeah, and tomorrow is going to be another long day. We're both going to need to be on our toes."

They rose in tandem and walked in silence back to the house. As they made their way through it, Chance turned off the lights and checked to make sure doors and windows were locked. She wondered if he'd done that every night before inheriting the kids and decided he probably hadn't. Endicott, Indiana, didn't exactly seem like a hotbed of crime, and he was a big strapping man who could take care of himself. With little ones in the picture, though, she supposed you could never be too careful.

At the foot of the steps, they paused to part ways. His bedroom for now would be the sofa, and he'd already moved the sheets from his bed down to it, along with, she couldn't help noting, a pair of still-folded-up sweatpants. A pair of sweatpants and no shirt. Which meant Chance would be sleeping in sweatpants and no shirt. She wondered if the sweatpants were a new addition to his nightly routine, too, then decided she should probably just stop thinking. Unfortunately, that no-shirt thing had wedged itself into her brain pretty well, and she feared it probably wasn't going to go away anytime soon. Maybe she should have another glass of wine...

"Good night, Poppy," he said softly, gazing down at her from what seemed like a million miles away. He was as tall as he was handsome. Damn him.

"Good night, Chance," she replied, just as quietly.

For a moment, they only looked at each other in silence, as if neither wanted to be the first to turn away. Then, finally, and with one last smile, Chance did. As he approached the sofa, he started unbuttoning his shirt, which was, without question, Poppy's signal to run away as fast as she could and never look back. Instead, she took the stairs slowly, one by one, gazing over her shoulder as she went, holding her breath until the big reveal, which, when it happened, was... Wow. Breathtaking. Even in the scant light, she could see the bump and curve of every salient muscle on his back and arms, and her mouth went dry. But once she got to the top of the stairs, she could no longer see down into the living room. Not unless she got down on all fours and scrunched up her body into an odd angle to peer through the balustrade. Which she actually started to do before catching herself and making herself stop.

Bed, she told herself again. She should be in bed. *Without* Chance, she further clarified to herself, since she seemed to need that clarification. She also needed sleep. Among other things. She just had to be sure it was sleep she focused on and not the other things, since that way lay madness.

She paused briefly at the kids' room to make sure they were asleep, then headed to her temporary bedroom. If only she were okay herself, everything would be fine. But having met Chance Foley—and seen all the muscles on his back and arms—and having discovered more than a few things about herself today, she feared she would never be okay again.

Most troubling of all, though, was her realization that what she had been thinking was totally okay all her life might not be okay at all.

Chapter Six

It was still dark when Poppy's alarm went off the next morning, but that was nothing new. She was generally at the office by 7:30 a.m., and even if she wasn't in Boston today, she still had work to do. Having slept with the window open, however—because it was a nice night, and she was never able to do that at home—the room was a tad chilly, and she hadn't packed a robe. She glanced at Chance's closet. She didn't want to snoop, of course, but maybe he wouldn't mind if she borrowed a shirt?

She grabbed the first long-sleeved one she saw, a soft gray flannel that fell past her hips, and rolled up its sleeves until she found her hands. Then she gathered her tablet from the nightstand where she'd left it the night before after making a few more notes before turning out the light. She paused briefly by the door to the children's room to check on them—they were both still out cold—then ambled silently down to the kitchen. And—all right, all right—she also checked briefly on Chance on her way to find that he was also sound asleep, lying on his back with a sturdy arm thrown over his head, the sheet having dipped low enough to reveal all the glorious muscles she'd only been able to imagine last night. In a word, *Oh, baby.* Which, okay, was two words, but one just wasn't enough for a torso like that.

Probably best she move on to the kitchen.

She was grateful to discover Chance was one of those people who set up the coffee maker the night before, and even more grateful that it was a model that didn't require a lot of thought to figure out which button was the On. Normally, she was pretty clearheaded and alert when she woke up in the mornings. But normally, she didn't spend the day before herding two unruly children, and her dreams the night before weren't filled with a shirtless mouthwatering Adonis who looked a lot like Chance Foley.

Oh, who was she kidding? It had totally been Chance filling her dreams last night. And in a lot of those dreams—

Ahem. She wondered if he had half-and-half for the coffee. And sugar. She could really use some sugar this morning.

A search of the fridge offered no half-and-half, but he did have whole milk—probably purchased with the kids in mind—which would do fine. A quick cabinet search revealed a small container of sugar. She also found a loaf of whole grain bread and some fresh fruit, which, in addition to reassuring her yet again that Chance was going to do a good job with the kids, also took care of breakfast.

By the time Poppy was fully refueled, the sun was starting to creep up over the trees. She'd planned to just go back to bed to work for a while but, unable to help herself, she instead took her second cup of coffee and tablet out onto the patio.

It was a glorious morning, with just a touch of autumn in the air. The woods behind the house were alive with the happy chirping of what sounded like thousands of birds, and a trio of deer stood at the very edge of the woods, watching her. She moved carefully to the chair she'd occupied the night before so as not to startle them, but they went easily back to their grazing. Clearly, this was a regular stop on their morning rounds, and they felt in no way threatened. She inhaled a deep breath, filling her nose with the sweet aroma of damp earth and withering leaves, and she reminded herself that this was only temporary, so she needed to stop enjoying it *so much*.

She knew a moment of envy when she realized Chance woke up to this every morning. In Boston, she awoke to the sounds of car alarms and garbage trucks and the aromas of diesel and dumpster. And the only wildlife she ever encountered were pigeons and squirrels and her building doorman, Corky.

She wasn't sure how long she worked before she heard the creak of the back door opening, but when she looked up again, the deer had disappeared, the birds had quieted, the sun was well above the trees and Chance was half naked. Um, that was to say, Chance was standing on the patio, wearing only the sweatpants he'd slept in the night before. So maybe he was actually half dressed. Which was a subtle and pretty much meaningless clarification, but somehow Poppy needed to make it to herself, because the last time she'd seen him half naked, he'd been in bed. The difference was night and day—literally—where the day version of Chance meant doing harmless things like going to fun fairs with children and the night version of Chance meant, um, something else completely.

"Good morning," he said as he lifted a cup of coffee to his lips. In her dreams last night, those lips had done things to her that were nothing short of miraculous. But, wow, had her dreams been wrong about the rest of him. He was way more sculpted and chiseled and brawny and powerful and hard and unyielding and—

Well, anyway, he looked even better in real life than he had in her dreams. And seeing how nearly every muscle in his torso danced—truly danced—when he lowered his cup and began to stride toward her made something in Poppy start dancing, too. A lot.

"Good morning," she replied, her voice coming out dry and hoarse for some reason.

He took the chair opposite hers. "Nice shirt."

She looked down at the garment she'd pilfered from his closet. "I hope you don't mind. It was a little chilly when I got up."

He waved a hand dismissively, making his abdominal muscles do the poetry-in-motion thing again. She tried not to fall out of her chair.

"My house is your house," he said. Then, with a grin, he added, "It looks better on you than it does on me."

Well, yeah. That was because, on him, it covered up all that glorious flesh and sinew. All she said, however, was "Thanks." And she hoped she wasn't blushing when she said it. Though she suspected she was. Because—duh—glorious flesh and sinew.

"How long have you been up?" he asked.

She glanced at the time on her tablet. "A few hours."

"You get up even earlier than me. Well, on days when I have to work," he added. "Like a lot of folks, I closed up shop this week, in light of the comet festival. Worked out well with the kids coming. Schools are out this week, too, so they'll have a little time to get used to being here before they have to be thrown into that."

"Well, my paralegal comes in at six so that she can leave at three to pick up her kids at school. I wanted to talk to her about a few things with the case before she got too deep into her day."

"Right. Your case. I keep forgetting you have a lot of work to do this week. Thanks again for staying."

"It shouldn't be too big a problem," she assured him. "The bulk of the work is done. Mostly what's left is the fine-tuning."

He sipped his coffee and eyed her thoughtfully, and she wondered what he was thinking.

"You have a wonderful home here," she said impulsively. "When I first came out this morning, there were actually deer back there."

"Yeah, it's a nature preserve, totally protected. No hunting or camping or anything like that, but it's great for hiking and exploring. Deer show up

pretty regularly in the yard. Along with foxes, rac-
coons, coyotes…"

"Coyotes?" she interrupted, alarmed. "You have
coyotes here?"

"Don't worry," he hurried to reassure her. "They're
pretty skittish animals. They won't be a danger to the
kids. But they do show up often enough that people
know to keep an eye on their small pets." As if to
further relieve her fears, he added, "There are wild
turkeys and grouse in the yard sometimes, too. And
bats at night. The kids ought to love seeing those."

Poppy was sure they would. Their life here was
going to be so different from the one they would
have had in Boston. If they had to lose their parents, at least there would be some small reward in
having a place like this to grow up.

"I think, ultimately, they're going to be very
happy here, Chance," she said.

"I hope you're right."

She knew she was. Mostly because she realized
how happy she herself would have been to grow up
in a place like this. Weird, considering the house
she'd called home as a child was practically a Boston landmark and was the very definition of old
money and old-world luxury. Who needed a backyard like this when there was an original John Con-
stable landscape hanging in your father's study?
Who needed to listen to a chorus of birds every

morning when your parents had loge seating at the Boston Symphony Orchestra? Who needed a breakfast of toast, fruit and coffee with a gorgeous man on the side when your family had a personal chef famous for her arugula and pistachio pesto quiche?

Unless maybe it was a little girl who had longed for more than perfunctory and conditional attention from her parents? Yeah, maybe.

Chance sipped his coffee thoughtfully, then looked at her again. "Do you think the kids are okay?" he asked. "I mean, with their parents' being gone? I'm not sure how a six-year-old processes death and grief. I don't know what to say to them about it."

"I think they're doing as well as can be expected," Poppy told him. "I did some reading on the subject, and at their age, kids are still learning to understand death and might get confused about it. Don't be surprised if they withdraw or get too clingy. They might have nightmares or good dreams about their parents. They might eat too much or not eat enough."

"Well, gee, that's super helpful," he said wryly.

"Take your cues from them," she said. "Don't bring up the subject unless they do, and when they do, be as honest as you can. They were at their parents' memorial service, but we didn't tell them about their parents' cremation. That seems like a subject for conversation when they're older. But I'm reasonably sure they know their parents aren't coming back."

He nodded, sighed and sipped his coffee again. She wished she could offer him more sound advice. But she didn't know any more about children's grief than he did. She didn't know anything about adult grief, for that matter. Poppy had never lost anyone to death who was close to her. Of course, that might have been because she rarely let anyone get too close. Icy, ruthless, cutthroat heart and all that.

"I was wondering," Chance said, "if I should find a child psychologist or something for them to talk to. There are times when I think maybe I would have benefited from something like that after my dad's death."

"I had them speak to a counselor a couple of times before we left Boston," Poppy told him. "She said they seemed to be processing things normally, but to be prepared for now for sudden outbursts of grief that might come out of nowhere."

Chance stared into his coffee, but only replied softly, "Noted."

Poppy lifted a hand to reach out to him, but realized he was sitting too far away from her to make contact. So she dropped her hand into her lap again. "Normally," she said, "the kids would find comfort in going back to their routines, but their routines are shot to hell, so that's not really going to apply here. Maybe help them find a new routine. If they want to talk, listen to them. Validate their feelings. Make sure they feel safe. Comfort them when they need it."

He nodded again. Somehow, though, Poppy got the feeling Chance, too, was confused about his brother's death and needed to feel safe and comforted. But his routine was as shot to hell as the kids' routines were. She wished she knew what to say to him that would make everything okay. But she didn't.

So she only told him, "The children are lucky to have you."

He had been about to sip his coffee again, but for some reason lowered his cup. She waited for him to say something, but he didn't. He only looked at her with a lot more scrutiny than she found comfortable, as if he were reading something into her words that simply was not there.

"I'm going to need to do some shopping today," she said in an effort to change the subject. Because, for some reason, the subject suddenly needed to be changed. "I didn't bring enough for a near-week's stay. Just my work and travel clothes and no toiletries." Not to mention only two pairs of underwear.

Which she wouldn't mention. Because that way lay more madness. "It shouldn't take long."

"That's fine," Chance said. "It'll give me a chance to introduce the kids to Endicott. And who knows? They might need a few things, too."

Endicott's historic district, which doubled as its commercial district and tripled, for now, as Comet Festival Central, was hopping when Chance and Poppy and the kids arrived later that morning to— he tried not to gag on the word—*shop*. He couldn't remember ever *shopping* in his life. If he needed something, he bought it online at one of a handful of places where he bought everything. Mostly, though, he made do with what he had. He was a man of simple needs and didn't conspicuously consume if he didn't have to. At least, that was how it used to be. With two growing kids, though— he'd swear the twins were taller this morning than they'd been when they went to bed last night—he would doubtless be contributing to the gross national product on a much more regular basis from here on out.

"Does the foot traffic ever slow down?" Poppy asked as the four of them made way for yet another group of revelers, these dressed as satellites, as best he could tell, in shiny silver tunics and fluttering tinfoil…stuff. She herself was wearing the same outfit she'd worn the day before, right down to the pearls, and he figured she was eager to replace her clothes with something more suited to both the festival and what was promising to be a warm day.

"On a normal day, yes," Chance told her. "But not during the Comet Festival. Especially not this week." He looked at the kids and smiled. "Get your wishes ready for Bob's Thursday night pass. That's when you're going to want to make them."

Finn and Quinn exchanged excited looks. They'd been surprisingly cheerful and cooperative so far this morning. Yes, the day was young, but they hadn't thrown a single pancake at breakfast, and no syrup or jam had left the table except to go into their mouths. Though they did call Poppy *Poopy* a few times after she took away a box of matches they'd found in a drawer Chance hadn't opened in months—which made him check every other drawer in the kitchen for potential hazards. In spite of the name-calling, he was hopeful that maybe their less-than-stellar behavior yesterday had been an anomaly.

"Uncle Chance!" Quinn suddenly shouted at the top of her lungs. "That fat guy behind you farted! It smells horrible!"

Or not.

Chance didn't want to turn around. But, damn,

he was learning how parenting came with a lot of unexpected—and not particularly pleasant—responsibilities and so, reluctantly, he did. He offered the man, who was neither fat, nor smelly, a thin smile, taking in the guy's purple alien unitard costume and the sauerkraut-covered kielbasa he was shoving into his mouth.

"Sorry," he said. "Kids. Social skills are always a work in progress."

The alien glared at the group and strode away, his glittery deely bobbers sparkling in the late morning sun. Chance turned back to give his niece a stern look.

"Quinn," he said evenly, "that was unbelievably rude. You should know better than to call someone fat and say they smell bad. How would you feel if someone called you stinky?"

"But I'm not stinky," she said.

Chance stood his ground. "No, you're not. But how would you feel if someone called you that?" he repeated.

Quinn glared at him even harder than the alien had. Then, after a moment, her expression softened. "Not very good," she said grudgingly.

"So do you understand now why you shouldn't say mean things like that?"

"I guess…"

As the group made their way down Water Street

toward a block of shops where he knew Poppy would be able to find everything she'd need for the next few days, Chance added a little more to the lesson. He assured Quinn it was okay to think whatever she wanted—though he would hope she didn't think mean things about people, either—and encouraged enough back-and-forth between the two of them to give her the opportunity to figure out for herself how words and actions had repercussions. Then he patted himself on the back for completing a session of halfway decent parenting and sent a silent thank-you up to his own parents for being such good examples and giving him something to model himself after.

Then Finn tripped over a crack in the sidewalk and nearly fell, shouting at the top of his lungs the epithet he'd learned from Lionel the day before, something that drew the disapproving eye of every other person around them. Chance realized then that one small session of halfway decent parenting wasn't nearly enough for him to be congratulating himself for anything.

He looked at Poppy, who was trying very hard not to laugh, and gestured toward the next block. "There are a bunch of shops down that way for you—and Quinn, too, if she wants to go with you." Then he pointed in the other direction. "In the meantime, Finn and I are going to sit down on that bench over there and have a conversation about the English language."

Poppy looked at Quinn. "What do you say? You want to help me pick out some things? We might even find a thing or two for you, too."

Quinn nodded enthusiastically, and the two of them were off. Chance looked down at his nephew with disapproval.

"What?" Finn said. "People say that word all the time."

Yeah, they did. Chance had said it himself a time or two. Or ten. Thousand. That was beside the point. The point was that he was never ever going to say it again. In front of the kids.

"C'mon. Let's talk," he told Finn, guiding him toward the bench.

Poppy made short work of her shopping list, thanks to the concentration of boutiques in Endicott's shopping district and, she had to admit, the help of Quinn. In spite of her tomboy ways, the little girl was enchanted by places like the bath shop, where she steered Poppy away from the clean scents like the rosemary and bamboo she would normally buy and filled their basket instead with gardenia soap and jasmine shampoo and little soaps shaped like starfish and mermaids, which Quinn insisted she needed for herself. It was the same story in the lingerie shop, where Quinn's enchantment with the pastels and laces of some of the garments made Poppy gravitate away from the cotton panties and no-frills bras she usually wore to purchase more delicate pieces instead.

The last shop they entered was so Poppy could pick up some casual clothes more appropriate for her stay in Endicott. Normally, when she shopped for clothing, she went for bland, because that meant no one formed opinions about her based on her appearance. In her profession, she couldn't afford to have others—other attorneys or judges or juries— deciding in advance that she was too conservative or too progressive or too timid or too bold or too anything else. Inevitably, blandness had filtered into her everyday wear, too.

But there didn't seem to be any bland stores in Endicott. There were only adorable boutiques filled with the trendy or quirky. Like the one she and Quinn found called Valerie's Vintage. There, however, she discovered a section in the back beneath a handwritten sign that said What Would Jackie Wear? So Poppy was at least able to find some time- less, well-tailored pieces à la Jackie Kennedy, and that suited her just fine.

After paying for her purchases, she ducked back into one of the fitting rooms to throw on a pair of pale blue capris and a sleeveless button-up shirt spat- tered with midcentury modern starbursts. After slipping flat sandals on her feet, she tossed her clothes from the day before in with the rest of her new things and headed out.

"How do I look?" she asked Quinn.

In spite of the camaraderie the two of them had shared for the last hour, Poppy halfway expected some snarky remark, followed by an overly emphasized *Poopy*.

Instead, Quinn told her, "You look really pretty."

Poppy waited for a zinger to punctuate the compliment. But it never came. So she only said, "Thanks."

Quinn smiled a devilish smile, one Poppy recognized too well from her days with the children. Here came the zinger now, she thought. Quinn was about to say something snide. The little girl opened her mouth and inhaled to make a comment that was sure to offend, then looked thoughtful for a moment and suddenly snapped her mouth shut.

"What?" Poppy asked, anyway.

"Nothing," Quinn said. Then, almost apologetically, she added, "It was mean. I shouldn't say it out loud."

Well, way to go, Uncle Chance, Poppy thought. Until she realized there was still something about her attire that Quinn didn't like, and she was just insecure enough to want to know what it was.

"Just say it in a way that's not mean," she told the little girl.

"I like the other shirt better," Quinn told her. "The orange one."

"Coral," Poppy corrected her. "That color is called coral."

"If you say so."

It occurred to her then that she was currently doing the sort of thing most adult women did with other women their own age. *Friends*, she thought. That was the word she was looking for. Normally, adult women shopped with other adult women whom they considered friends. But Poppy was shopping with a child. One who, for that matter, had more interesting taste in clothing and accessories than she had herself. Of course, Quinn was one of only three people she knew in Endicott, but that was just it. There was no one in Boston Poppy would be doing her shopping with, regardless of age. She had no friends to do things like this with. She only had colleagues at work and a sister who felt more like, well, a colleague at work.

She pushed the realization away. It didn't matter. Friends and social situations only kept a person from achieving her full potential at her job. Having friends was almost as problematic as having a family.

"Is there anything else we need?" she asked Quinn.

The little girl shook her head.

"Then let's go find the boys, shall we?"

Chapter Seven

Chance and Finn were in the model-train shop when Poppy texted to tell him she and Quinn were finished shopping and asked where to meet them. Tucker's Trains 'n' Things had been an Endicott fixture for as long as Chance could remember and had been his and Logan's favorite place to go with their dad, who had been a model-train enthusiast. Their dad's trains had been the only interest the Foley brothers had in common—truth be told, the one thing they could share with camaraderie and without incident. Chance hadn't been in Tucker's since his father's death. It just hadn't felt right to go into the shop without his dad and, over the years, he'd put thoughts of his father's trains out of his head. But when Finn had seen the shop, he'd immediately grabbed his uncle's wrist and dragged him inside.

The two of them had spent the better part of an hour just looking at all the sets and weren't even halfway through them when Poppy and Quinn arrived. His niece immediately found her brother and joined him, and Poppy approached Chance.

Little about Tucker's had changed in the two decades since he was last here. There was still the incessant clickety-clack-clackity-click of the antique trains circling overhead and the steady hum of the newer electric ones on the tables. There was still the scent of dust and motor oil hovering over everything. There was still Mr. Tucker sitting on his stool in the corner, wearing his greasy canvas apron and big magnifying glass spectacles as he worked on someone's broken train. In spite of some of the troubling memories the place roused, Chance had to admit it was kind of nice to be back.

"This place is amazing," Poppy told him.

She'd changed into some of her new clothes and looked more comfortable and relaxed than she had the day before. It was hard to believe barely twenty-four hours had passed since he'd met her. Chance felt as if a lifetime had passed since yesterday morning. And he felt as if he'd known Poppy for a lifetime, too.

"This was one of my favorite places to come as a kid," he told her.

"I've never even thought about toy trains, but I can see why they're such a big thing for a lot of people."

"My dad was one of them," Chance said. "Our basement was filled with different sets. My favorite was a replica of some station in Moscow he visited when he was in college. Kazansky Station," he said when the name popped into his head clear as day. Funny that he would remember that so quickly. "It was pretty awesome."

"Do you still have it?"

He shook his head. "My mom sold all my dad's trains to a dealer in Indianapolis after his death."

Poppy's astonishment was obvious when she replied, "Why would she do that when she had two sons who would have probably loved having them?"

"We totally would have," Chance assured her. "But I think she just couldn't stand the thought of seeing them every day and being reminded of my dad."

"She still could have just boxed them up and saved them for you."

"I don't think she even considered that. She was hit pretty hard by his death. We all were. I mean, it just came out of nowhere. We were so unprepared."

When Poppy said nothing in response, Chance

turned to look at her and found her looking at him, too. Her expression revealed nothing of what she might be thinking, but he could pretty much tell, anyway. Shane Foley's death had been the beginning of the end of the Foley family. None of them had realized it at the time, of course, but the three remaining family members never quite felt like the same family again. Poppy was probably feeling sorry for all of them in that moment. So was Chance, for that matter. But—

"Life goes on, you know?" he said quietly. "It was fine that she let the trains go to someone else. It wouldn't have been the same for Logan and me, anyway, having them without Dad."

"Maybe not," Poppy said. "But it was a tradition you could have carried on in some way."

The Foleys of Endicott hadn't had many traditions. Or any, now that Chance thought about it. Yeah, they'd embraced the traditional trappings of the major holidays, but those were universal traditions, not Foley ones. Poppy was right, though. His dad's trains were a little out of the ordinary, and they'd all loved them with a singular passion. It was kind of a shame he hadn't been able to pick up where his father left off and keep building that world. Especially now that there was another generation of Foleys that might enjoy it.

Poppy looked at the twins, who had moved to

another train layout and were chattering with much excitement. "Looks like Quinn and Finn take after their grandfather."

The statement caught Chance off guard. All this time, he'd been thinking about how much the twins took after his brother, Logan. It had never occurred to him that there were strands of his own father—and mother, too, of course—woven into their DNA. He remembered how after losing his dad, he'd always gravitated toward books and games and movies whose protagonists were immortal, and how he'd always been vaguely resentful that such people didn't exist in real life. But maybe immortality did exist in a way. Because his niece and nephew had parts inside them of people who were long gone. Of the people Chance had loved most in the world.

"I wish I still had my dad's old set," he said suddenly, softly.

He didn't realize he'd spoken aloud until Poppy replied, "Maybe you and the kids could start one of your own."

For a moment, he warmed to the idea. They could do it today. Buy a good starter set and assemble it in his basement, the way his dad had done in theirs. Then, every year for Christmas or the kids' birthdays, Chance could buy them another piece to contribute to it, like his folks had done for him and Logan. Maybe, eventually, they, like he and Logan, could do some chores around the house and yard for a few bucks and they could spend it here at Tucker's, the way the Foley boys had when their dad brought them in once a week on allowance day. Finn and Quinn could build their own locomotive world, one piece at a time under Chance's guidance, the same way he and Logan had built theirs with their dad's help. It could go a long way toward replacing the set his father had built so lovingly over the years. And it wouldn't just be rebuilding the train set he'd lost as a child. In a way, it would almost be like they were rebuilding the entire Foley fami—

"Yeah, that's probably not a good idea," he told Poppy, his voice even softer than before.

As if Finn and Quinn had heard him speak—which was impossible, because the cacophony in the store was considerable—the twins glanced up at Chance and smiled. He waited for the ripple of unease he'd felt yesterday when their laughter had reminded him of a horror movie. Instead, he found himself smiling back. They pulled themselves away from the train set and joined him and Poppy.

"Can we come back here another day?" Quinn asked hopefully.

That wasn't a good idea, either, Chance decided on the spot. But both kids were looking at him so earnestly, all he could say in reply was "Sure." Then, in a long-overdue effort to change the subject, he asked Poppy and Quinn, "Did you all find everything you need?"

Poppy opened her mouth to reply, but Quinn beat her to it. "She got four shirts and three pairs of pants, a dress and some sandals. And some shampoo that smells like jasmine."

Poppy looked more than a little uncomfortable. Chance was intrigued. Though why would she feel uneasy about smelling like jasmine? He didn't even know what it was.

"The bath-shop selection was a bit thin," she said by way of an explanation.

"No, it wasn't," Quinn interjected. "They had lots of stuff."

"Um, I mean…" Poppy backtracked. "Quinn picked it out for me. I don't usually go for florals. They don't suit me at all."

Chance looked at his niece for confirmation. Quinn nodded. "It smells really pretty," she said.

He looked back at Poppy. "Then florals obviously suit you perfectly," he said. Flirtatiously. Which was weird, because Chance normally—manfully—avoided flirtatiousness. Flirtation. Flirting. Whatever it was called. See? He normally so manfully avoided it, he wasn't even sure what it was.

Um, where was he?

Oh, yeah. He was looking at Poppy. And thinking about how pretty she was. And noticing that she was actually smiling at him having told her she was pretty, as if she really liked that he had said it. So maybe he was jumping the gun a bit on avoiding the whole flirting thing and should try it more often. He added it to the day's to-do list.

"And you should see the underwear she bought," Quinn hurried on with a giggle. "There's some that are pink with little hearts."

Chance laughed, too. "Really? Well, that sounds very, ah…"

Poppy threw him a warning look.

"Pink," he finally said. "It sounds very pink."

"Quinn picked those out, too," Poppy stated emphatically.

This time, the warning look she threw was at the little girl. Quinn, however, didn't seem to notice. "There are some other ones that are purple with butterflies," she volunteered enthusiastically. "And some black ones that—"

That was when Poppy gently but firmly placed her hand over Quinn's mouth to stifle anything else the girl might say. Which had promised to be a lot, because Quinn kept mumbling in spite of the impediment, and Chance would have given his right arm just then to know what she was saying.

With all the dignity of a Victorian governess, Poppy announced, "It's always good to have a variety of light and dark colors among one's underthings. One never knows where one's wardrobe might take one."

Spoken like a woman who had no idea what the future—or, at least, the week ahead—held. Which was more than a little interesting coming on the heels of what he'd just discovered about the whole flirting thing and the whole underwear thing. Maybe Chance should buy some new underwear, too. Just in case his wardrobe—or something—took him someplace surprising this week, too.

"Okay, then," he said to the group, "since we're in town, if you guys are interested, I could show you where I work. We could even take the boat out for a little while this afternoon if you want. I invited my friends Felix and Max to come over and grill burgers tonight, because they want to meet you all, but between now and then, we can do whatever you want. So. What would you like to do?"

Poppy sat at the end of a battered pier with her bare feet dangling in the waters of the Ohio and watched Chance throw Finn into the river a third time.

The boy squealed with laughter before a resounding splash silenced him, then started yelling, "Do it again," the minute his head broke the surface.

"My turn next!" Quinn shouted as she paddled

alongside her brother, racing him to see who could make it back to the pier first.

The day that had started off so glorious that morning had only grown more beautiful the higher the sun climbed in the sky. True to his word, Chance had shown them around the shop where he built and repaired boats, patiently answering the children's million questions and letting them climb in and out of his various works in progress. Then they'd all clambered into the gorgeous vintage wooden Chris-Craft he'd rebuilt—practically from scratch, he'd explained—and headed out onto the river.

Poppy had boated pretty much all her life. Her family owned both a fifty-foot power yacht, dubbed *Mare Clausum* by their maritime-law-practicing father, that they berthed at Boston Yacht Club and a forty-foot sloop, *Mare Liberum*, that they kept for use at their cottage on Cape Cod. But neither of those massive, majestic vessels was anywhere near as beautiful as Chance's nineteen-foot runabout, *Ginger*. And watching him pilot it down the Ohio, the wind rushing through his dark hair, the sun beating down on his face, the complete joy in his expression at the prospect of being behind the wheel… Well, suffice to say, he was pretty gorgeous himself.

"Who's Ginger?" she asked, tilting her head toward the boat as Chance sat himself down on the pier beside her.

"My mom," he said.

Her father had named their boats after legal terms he used in his work. Chance had named his after his mother. His mom, she corrected herself. He'd called his mother *Mom*. She called her mother *Mother*. No way could Delilah Digby be confused for a mom.

As the children went looking for interesting rocks, Chance cautioned them to stay within view. He'd been barefoot since he boarded the boat, but now he rolled up the legs of his khakis to just below his knees and slung his feet into the water, too. Then he leaned back on his strong arms and tipped his head back, closing his eyes as the sun beat down upon them. His navy blue polo stretched taut across his chest, and she told herself she only imagined the ripple of muscles beneath the fabric. But she could imagine them very well. Because she still couldn't chase from her brain the memory of him sitting half naked on the patio that morning.

"You know, if I could spend every day like this," he said quietly, "I'd be the happiest man alive."

Poppy didn't doubt it. He looked absolutely sublime.

He opened his eyes and looked at her. "I don't

know how you city folks do it. I'd suffocate living in a place like Boston."

She grinned. "We have a river, too, you know. And boats."

He grinned back. "Do tell."

"Have you ever been to Boston?" she asked.

"I have, actually. A couple times. It's a great city—don't get me wrong. There's a ton of stuff to see and do. But that's kind of the problem. There's so much to see and do, I don't think I could ever see or do all of it. And there are so many people, where do you even begin? And it's so big. Way too much ground to cover."

"Those are the reasons I like it," Poppy told him.

Not that she ever really saw or did much outside of work. Or ran into many people other than coworkers. Or wandered into many areas of town other than the ones where she worked and lived.

"Different strokes," he said. "If I lived in a place like that, I'd wake up every morning feeling anxious and go to bed every night feeling overwhelmed."

Oh, and she didn't? Even so, it was a small price to pay for the lifestyle she had. Or, rather, the lifestyle she *would* have, in the not-too-distant future, when she made partner.

"You must find Endicott pretty pedestrian," he said.

"No, I think it's adorable," she replied honestly.

"But," he pressed.

"But," she echoed, "I'm not sure how people who live in small towns stay stimulated and engaged. I guess I'm just one of those people who needs to be anxious and overwhelmed in order to get anything done."

He gazed at her thoughtfully for a moment, and she really wished she could tell what he was thinking. Finally, he said, "That doesn't sound like a fun way to live."

"What does fun have to do with living?"

He started to laugh, then realized she was serious. "Fun and living aren't mutually exclusive," he told her. "In fact, there are a lot of people who would say fun and living are one and the same."

"Not where I come from."

"Then you need to reevaluate your origins."

Tell her something she didn't already know. The problem was that her origins were so deeply rooted there was no way to reevaluate them without renting a backhoe and digging a whole lot deeper than she was willing to dig. That far down, things got pretty dark and dirty. Best not to poke around too much.

"If I'd known we were going out on your boat today," she said, "I would have had the kids bring their swimsuits."

"Yeah, sorry about that. It was kind of a spur-of-the-moment idea. But kids don't mind swimming in their clothes. We did it all the time when we were their age."

"Well, maybe you did."

He looked surprised. "Really? You never swam in your clothes?"

"Are you kidding? I never wanted to go into the water even when I did have a bathing suit on."

"Okay, how can you grow up in a major boating mecca like New England and not be swimming all summer long?"

"Oh, I love being on the water," she assured him. "I just don't like being *in* the water."

Probably because, when she was a little girl, her brother Barnaby's favorite thing to do whenever they were near the water was to toss her off any given pier or over the side of their boat even though she was a notoriously bad swimmer. And her sister Odette's favorite thing to do on those occasions was to laugh at Poppy flailing about as she tried to get back. And her parents' favorite thing to do was to sigh in disappointment that their youngest child wasn't the champion swimmer that her sister and brother both were.

Good times.

"I just don't like to swim," she told Chance. "And I will do *anything* to avoid going into the water."

"Well, I'll try not to hold that against you," he told her. "Me, if I can't be on the boat, I want to be in the water. And if I can't be in the water, I want to be on the boat. Shame I have to work for a living. Still, as jobs go, mine's pretty sweet."

Poppy wanted to argue that hers was, too, but something stopped her. Yes, she enjoyed what she did—she *did*—and she couldn't imagine doing anything else. But if, on a day like this, she could do it outdoors and at her own pace? That would indeed be pretty sweet.

She looked out at the river then and saw something floating by about a hundred feet out. It looked like a box or laundry basket, bobbing slowly up and down. Bad enough people had to throw litter into a perfectly lovely waterway, but when they hurled oversize pieces like that in, it was criminal. She cupped a hand over her eyes to see if she could tell what it was and saw something inside it move. Then a tiny head popped up over the side. A tiny head with huge floppy ears. And it started barking.

"Oh, my god!" she cried, jumping to her feet. "There's a dog out there in the water!" Without even thinking about what she was doing, she jumped feetfirst into the river and began swimming— badly—toward the box.

She heard a splash behind her and knew Chance was following. Then she heard Quinn and Finn on the shore, calling out encouragement. Chance caught up with her just as she reached the box.

There was indeed a puppy inside, and he…she…
it…looked terrified. But when Poppy braced her
arms under the box to steady it, the puppy yipped
nervously and slathered her face with its tongue.
And even though her concern was keeping Little
Mister or Miss Doggo safe and dry, she couldn't
quite quell the shiver that wound through her when
Chance slipped a strong arm around her waist and
started swimming them all back to shore.

By the time they reached dry land, the puppy was
howling joyfully, the children were dancing with
excitement, Chance was tightening his hold on her
waist to help her out of the water and Poppy was
ready to swoon. Instead, she hugged the box to her
chest and collapsed onto the muddy ground. She
was immediately enveloped by the children, who
wanted to see/hold/cuddle/nuzzle/kiss the puppy,
but Poppy held them off for the moment, until she
could be sure the little guy or girl was okay.

"So much for doing *anything* to avoid going into
the water," Chance said with a chuckle as he sat
down beside her. "I think you just broke an Olym-
pic record out there."

"Who would do such a thing?" she demanded.
"What kind of scumbag tosses a puppy into a box
and sends it down the river like that? Find that scumbag, and give me five minutes alone with him."

The puppy, however, seemed fine, save probably

being hungry and thirsty. Poppy was no canine expert, but a quick glance under its tail revealed that *it* was a she. Further inspection seemed to suggest she was a mix of some kind of hound and terrier, and she'd clearly inherited the cutest bits of both gene pools.

Chance looked at the kids. "There are some bottles of water on the boat and some plastic cups. Puppy's probably thirsty. Could you please go grab one of each for me?"

The children nodded with much enthusiasm, then ran off to retrieve the requested items. Poppy gave the puppy a final once-over, then set her on the ground between herself and Chance. But she jumped right back into her lap and planted her muddy little paws on her chest, then showered her with kisses again.

"You're in trouble now," Chance said. "You're never gonna get rid of her. It's that old legend. If you save someone's life, you become responsible for it."

"There's no way I can be responsible for a puppy," she said. "Not only does my building not allow pets, but my lifestyle doesn't allow them, either."

"Maybe her being in the river was an accident," Chance said. "Maybe she actually belongs to someone who's missing her, and we just need to get her home."

Poppy shook her head. "You are such a nice person, always seeing the good in people."

He lifted a damp shoulder and let it drop. All of him was damp, from the dark hair he'd pushed back on his head to the thick eyelashes that looked even thicker when wet, and the polo was now clinging even more tightly to every muscle he possessed. Good god, the man was potent.

"No reason to go looking for the bad in people all the time," he told her. "If it's there, it'll come out soon enough."

The puppy barked in agreement. Dog logic and man logic evidently had a lot in common.

"We can take her to the vet and have her scanned," he continued. "She might belong to someone and just got out and got herself into trouble."

"And if that's not the case?" Poppy asked. "If she doesn't belong to anyone? If some scumbag really did send her down the river in a box, hoping to never see her again?"

The scuffle of little feet behind them announced the arrival of Quinn and Finn, just in time to hear her questions.

"Can we keep him?" they said as one. Okay, shouted as one.

Chance winced visibly at the question. *Can we keep him?* was doubtless right up there with *Where do babies come from?* when it came to questions parents dreaded to hear from their children. But all he said in reply was "He's a she."

"Can we keep her?" they repeated as one.

Chance bit back a groan. Poppy sympathized. Caring for a puppy would be like caring for another child. Worse. At least the kids were housebroken. "There's an awful lot of work that goes into taking care of a dog," he told the kids.

They looked at him as if he were an idiot for saying something like that. Of course, they pretty much looked at him and Poppy both as if they were idiots all the time.

Chance continued, "You'll have to take her out every morning to, you know, poop..."

The children giggled at that.

"And every night before you go to bed to, you know, pee..."

More giggling.

"You'll have to make sure she's fed," he continued. "Give her baths. Take her for walks. Play with her..."

Clearly, the children did not think any of those things were problems. "So can we keep her?" Finn asked again.

Chance sighed. Poppy smiled. He was such a pushover. "Yeah, okay. If no one claims her, we can keep her."

The children's ecstatic "Yay, yay, yay!" was punctuated by another dance along the water.

"She needs a name," Finn said. Shouted. Whatever.

"Pippi," Quinn suggested. Shouted. Whatever.

"Like Pippi Longstocking?" Poppy asked.

Quinn nodded. "Pippi the puppy that Poppy saved."

Chance laughed. "Someone had to say it."

Poppy glared at him as hard as she could, but he only laughed harder.

"Pippi the puppy that Poppy saved sounds fated to me," he said.

Poppy sighed. "*Fated*. That's one word for it."

The children filled a cup with water, then took turns holding it for Pippi to quench her thirst. By mutual consensus, the group decided to call it a day for river operations, especially when Chance mentioned they might be able to find a vet's office open where they could have the puppy scanned for a chip and checked out for any health problems.

By the time they made it back to his boatyard, Poppy's new clothes were covered with little muddy puppy prints, and every inch of her exposed skin was covered with puppy spit. She'd never had a puppy growing up. The Digbys had had dogs, but they were more her parents' pets than they were the Digby children's—two hulking, haughty mastiffs named Duke and Brumilda that were in no way inclined to play with children. And even if they had been, they probably would have crushed—or perhaps eaten—them. Pippi, on the other hand, seemed to be made of rubber and liked children very much.

Poppy would have thought she'd be annoyed that her new purchases and she herself were almost irreparably soiled. Instead, she couldn't stop laughing at Pippi's antics. And when they did, in fact, find a vet's office open, and when that vet happened to be a middle-school friend of Chance's, Pippi got right in to be checked over. After Pippi was given a clean bill of health and a round of shots—not to mention a chip proclaiming Quinn and Finn Foley as her new owners—the group tumbled back into Chance's Jeep and returned to his house, with just enough time for them all to clean up before his friends arrived for dinner.

And as Poppy stood in the shower, washing puppy and river grime off herself, she marveled at how much the four of them had done today, and how much they had seen, and how much distance they had traveled. And the day wasn't even close to being over, because she would be meeting new people tonight. Funny how only a couple of days in Endicott had filled her life with more, well, life than it had seen in a long time.

Or maybe that wasn't funny. Maybe that was…

something else. Something she didn't want to think about. Because she still had a lot to do today. A lot of people to meet. A lot of fun to have. And thoughts about her life in Boston had absolutely no place in that.

Chapter Eight

"Holy crow, she's wearing pearls."

"They belonged to her great-aunt. They're very special to her."

"Yeah, but who wears pearls to grill?"

Chance made a face at his friend Max, who was seated in one of the three Adirondack chairs on his patio. Their friend Felix sat in another one. It occurred to him that he was going to have to order a couple more of those for the kids. Both of his friends were gazing toward the back of the yard, where Poppy and the kids and Pippi the puppy had migrated almost immediately after the men's arrival. Felix and Max had been able to exchange all of a dozen words with the kids before they took off again, tearing out the back door, Pippi yipping happily behind them. They'd exchanged even fewer words with Poppy, because she'd run after them to keep them out of trouble. After grabbing a long-neck apiece from the fridge, the three men had followed out the back door and taken their usual places around the firepit.

Nothing about the current situation felt *usual* to Chance, however. Normally, when Max and Felix came over, they threw a few slabs of ribs on the grill, tipped back selections from Endicott's sole microbrewery with abandon and talked about things like the elegant silhouette of a Hutchinson boat, the hardiness of different spireas, and variations on ropa vieja. This evening, it would be burgers and hot dogs on the fire, the beers would be few and conversation would no doubt center on the passel of newcomers who were suddenly resident in Chance's home.

"Can you keep it down, please, Max?" he said in response to his friend's statement. "Poppy might hear you."

Though that wasn't likely, since she and the kids were too far away. As Pippi sniffed at everything she encountered, they were all sitting cross-legged in the grass in front of the honeysuckle bushes Chance should have pruned a month ago. Poppy seemed to be teaching them how to pull the honey-suckle stem through the flower to preserve a perfect bead of nectar on the other side that they could ingest and enjoy. He was kind of amazed it was something she knew how to do, since one, he wasn't sure honeysuckle even grew in Boston, and two, she didn't strike him as the type to have had a childhood that included that particular skill. Then again, maybe honeysuckle draining was just one of those instinctive things every kid knew to do, like chasing fireflies and catching snowflakes on their tongues.

"But she's wearing pearls to grill," Max insisted again. Clearly, to him, that was a major violation of the holy grill.

"She has on shorts and a T-shirt," Chance pointed out in her defense. "Kind of."

Okay, so they weren't actually shorts, but some kind of pants that ended just below her knees, and they were made of some kind of material that probably shouldn't be sitting in grass. And her T-shirt was actually a flowy, shimmering pink thing he would have expected to see on Oaks Day at Churchill Downs. Hey, it had short sleeves. Maybe it was a lowercase *t*, but it was still in the T-shirt family.

"I like the pearls," Felix said. "They're classy. She seems like a classy girl."

"Oh, don't let her hear you calling her a girl,"

Chance warned him. "She's an icy, ruthless, cut-throat attorney."

Felix considered her again. "She doesn't seem icy, ruthless and cutthroat."

"Well, she is," Chance assured him.

"How do you know?" Max asked.

"She told me so. Like six times already. And she's *this* close to becoming a partner in some tony Boston law firm. She told me that like six times, too." For some reason, he couldn't resist adding, "Not to mention I found out she's a year older than me."

Felix grinned back. "Whoa, going for older women now, are we?"

Chance grimaced. "Well, don't make it sound like I've only dated teenagers before this."

"Well, no, not teenagers," Max agreed. "But how old was your last girlfriend? Twenty-three?"

"She was not twenty-three," Chance assured him.

Felix laughed, too. "Yeah, remember, Max? She was twenty-three-*and-a-half*."

Chance cringed at the memory of Ellie saying exactly that at one point. All right, all right. So he didn't always go for the worldly, cultivated type. He didn't always go for young and inexperienced, either. He didn't discriminate at all when it came to women. And, hey, Ellie had owned her own fashion design business. Just because all her fashions had looked like Japanese schoolgirl uniforms didn't mean anything. It was an actual fashion trend. It even had a name. Ellie had told him so. Chance just couldn't remember what it was at the moment.

"Who I date is none of your business," Chance told the other men. Which totally wasn't true, because the three of them had spent their entire lives meddling in each other's crushes, then girlfriends, then lovers.

"So you and Poppy are dating?" Max asked with much interest.

"No," Chance replied immediately, emphatically. It surprised him, though, to realize how much it bothered him to say it. "Not unless you call trying to keep two little kids under control *dating*."

Felix muttered something in Spanish—probably one of his *abuela*'s pithy observances about life, the universe and everything—followed by, "*Mija*, you can call flower arranging a date if it involves spending time with someone."

"Flower arranging, huh?" Max replied with a smile.

Chance smiled, too. "Still trying to make time with Rory Vincent, I see," he said, grateful for the change of subject.

Rory Vincent had bought the flower shop next door to Felix's restaurant a few months ago, and ever since, Felix had been doing his best to engage her in romantic pursuits. Or, at least, what passed for romantic for a guy like Felix, who never seemed to stay interested in women for longer than it took for them to get interested in him. Rory, however, had been adamantly steering clear of him.

"I am not trying to make time with Rory Vincent," Felix denied. Not for the first time. And, not for the first time, Chance and Max both responded with knowing laughter.

"I'm not," he insisted. "She's my neighbor. I just want to be neighborly, that's all."

"Riiiight," Chance and Max chorused as one.

"Neighborly," Chance continued. "That's a new word for it."

Felix tipped back his beer with much gusto. "Besides," he said when he finished, "she seems to have picked up a stalker. I'm just trying to keep an eye on the situation. She's too nice a girl to deal with that."

"A stalker?" Chance echoed incredulously. "Do we have stalkers in Endicott?"

"Okay, maybe he's not a stalker," Felix conceded. "He's not very good at it. But you can't be too careful."

"Yeah, someone should tell Rory that about her next-door neighbor," Max said, still grinning.

"Hey, I hear Marcy Hanlon is back in town for the Comet Festival," Felix replied pointedly to

Max. Looked like Chance wasn't the only one who wanted to change the subject.

Max immediately sobered. "Yeah. She is."

Everyone in Endicott had heard Max's old high-school crush was back in town. And everyone knew she wasn't Marcy Hanlon anymore. Now she was Marcella Robillard, bestselling novelist and French viscountess. Well, everyone except Max knew that, since everyone in town had done their best to keep it under wraps, because it would destroy him to know Marcy had become such a glamorous gadabout married woman who would never, ever, return to Endicott under normal circumstances. Telling Max about that would have been like kicking a kitten.

"So you've seen her?" Chance asked cautiously.

Max nodded. "Ran into her at the bookstore yesterday. We only talked for a few minutes." He looked thoughtful—and not a little unhappy. "She's changed her looks a lot."

Oh, you have no idea how much she's changed, Chance thought. And he was going to make sure it stayed that way. Max, to this day, still carried a massive torch for Marcy. No way was Chance going to let her break his heart a second time.

"But we were talking about your girl," Max said, returning the subject to Chance and Poppy.

Not that he and Poppy were a subject he wanted

to return to. Hell, he and Poppy weren't even a subject.

"She's not a girl," he said again.

Felix smiled. "Yeah, especially not *your* girl, right?"

Except the way he said it, he absolutely meant to indicate that Poppy absolutely was Chance's girl. Which she wasn't. Absolutely.

"She's only in town for a few more days," he said. "And even that's only because of the kids, not me."

Felix and Max looked at Chance now with concern.

"So how's it going with the kids?" Max asked. "You guys gonna be okay?"

Chance sighed. "We're gonna have to be."

Felix looked back at Poppy and the kids again. They'd moved from sampling the honeysuckle to studying something in the grass. All three of them were on their hands and knees, and Quinn, in particular, seemed to be very interested in whatever they'd found. Finn, on the other hand, looked vaguely horrified. Pippi seemed a little cautious. Poppy was a mixture of all three. She was also getting her shimmery pants all muddy. And she didn't seem to care. One thing Chance would say for her— she was an interesting mix of…of a lot of…stuff.

"I still can't believe Logan got married and had

kids," Felix said. "He was like the antithesis of a family man."

"I still can't believe he never told me about them," Chance said. "I mean, I know he didn't leave town on the best of terms, and maybe he and I said some things to each other we shouldn't have, but..." He took another pull on his beer, still watching the kids. "I just wish he'd told me," he said again.

Quinn scooped up whatever the trio had been looking at, cupped one hand over the other and ran toward the three men.

"Uncle Chance!" she shouted on the way. "Look what we found!"

She drew up in front of him, smudged with dirt and out of breath. With a gentleness he would have sworn wasn't possible for her, she extended her hands toward him and, cautiously—another quality he was amazed to discover she possessed—lifted one. In the palm of the other sat the biggest, fattest, grossest grub he'd ever seen. He did his best not to gag.

"Wow," he said, hoping he sounded a lot more impressed than he felt. "That's...that's something."

"Hey, let me see," Max said.

Because if something came out of the ground, Max wanted to see it. He'd been that way since preschool. Quinn happily turned to show him her prize.

"Ooh, that's a beauty," he said with enthusiasm that was a lot more convincing than Chance's. Doubtless because it was genuine. "He'll be a Japanese beetle before long." Then, without missing a beat, he added, "Chance, you need to get your yard treated. I can do it next week."

Before Chance could thank him, Quinn interjected, "She. It's a girl."

Max looked ready to argue—did grubs even have genders?—but seemed to think better of it.

"I named her Zara," Quinn announced.

"Zara," Chance repeated. "I don't think I've ever met a grub named Zara."

"I named her after my friend Zara Faiza. She's in Brownies with me." She glanced up, looking at nothing, but seeming a little distressed. "I mean, she *was* in Brownies with me." Now she looked at Chance. "Can I do Brownies here, Uncle Chance?"

It was a simple question, but one that hit Chance like a brick. It honestly hadn't once occurred to him until that moment that the children would have left behind friends in Boston. That there would be people other than their parents that they were missing. But of course they would have had friends. Of course they would miss them. They'd had a whole life in Boston. He just hadn't been able to see past the immediacy of their current situation or been able to move outside of the moment since the kids arrived. Quinn had a friend named Zara. She probably had a lot of other friends, too. So did Finn, no doubt.

Chance made a mental note to ask Poppy about it after the kids were in bed tonight. Maybe he could set up a FaceTime or Zoom call for Quinn and Finn to visit their friends. And maybe, at some point, the three of them could pay a visit to Boston so they could see their friends in person again. And Poppy, too. He was sure the kids would love an opportunity to see Poppy again. And, okay, so would he.

He remembered Quinn was waiting for an answer to her question.

"Of course you can do Brownies," he said. "I'm sure there's a chapter at the school you and Finn will be attending."

"Troop," Quinn corrected him.

"Right," Chance replied. He looked at Finn, wanting to include him in the conversation. "What kind of stuff did you do up in Boston?"

"I played soccer," Finn said.

"We have that here," Chance assured him. "I know that for a fact, because Max here coaches a team."

"True dat," Max said. "My nephew's team. He's about your age. And there's always room on our roster for one more."

"I took guitar lessons," Quinn said.

"Her guitar is one of the things coming down with their furniture," Poppy told him.

"Hey, *mija*, I know a great guitar teacher," Felix interjected. "And you should downloand some stuff by Juanito Marquez. Dude's amazing."

Chance listened while the kids rattled off a half dozen or so other activities they'd engaged in before coming to Endicott and did some quick mental math. He could probably manage to drive them around to do all those things. Probably. Provided he organized his time wisely, quit his job and mastered the ability to travel through time, space and dimensions.

"Okay, so who wants a burger?" he asked in an effort to regain some small control of the situation. And he probably ought to get the grill going, since two growing kids had to be in bed a lot earlier than three single guys who refused to concede to the need for sleep.

The remainder of the night passed in a swirl of activity, bearing absolutely no similarity to the lazy late summer nights Chance had enjoyed in the past. As twilight settled, the children and puppy chased fireflies around the yard, their laughter a new sound in his environment. Not just because there had never been kids running around his house or yard, but because Finn and Quinn hadn't done a lot of laughing since their arrival. As apprehensive as he still was about the future, something about the sound reassured him. His life was never going to be the same, he knew. But maybe it wasn't going to be quite as turbulent as he'd initially feared. Maybe, just maybe, everything really would be all right.

It was nearing ten o'clock when Poppy finally got the children settled in bed with Pippi between them. Or, rather, into the sleeping bags that had originally belonged to their father and their uncle Chance. Though she suspected they predated even the Foley boys, because they were two oversize olive drab sacks lined with red-and-black flannel more reminiscent of their grandparents' time. Strange to think those sleeping bags were, in a way, the only heirlooms the children had. Adele's parents had been gone before she and Logan married and had left her with even less than he had. For children who had so much financial wealth, Quinn and Finn had so little in the way of family.

A pinch of guilt pricked the back of her brain. Poppy and Chance were the only family they had left. Half of their surviving family would be disappearing overnight with her return to Boston. And she had no idea when she would be able to get away to visit them again.

But what was she supposed to do? Chance would be far better at raising them than she would, and Endicott had more to offer them at this point in their lives than Boston did. Once the twins adjusted to their new life, they were going to flourish here. If Poppy were the one to take on their care, she'd have to hire a full-time nanny and squeeze them all into an urban condo where there would be no chasing fireflies or listening to birds or exploring woods. Her life in Boston was in no way suited to raising children, no matter how much she was starting to kind of wish it were.

She kissed Quinn and Finn on the forehead and told them good-night, then left the door ajar on her way out. As she descended the stairs, she heard Chance telling his friends good-night, then the click of the front door as it closed behind them. He had offered to help her put the kids to bed, but she'd told him to enjoy his time with his friends, knowing there wouldn't be many more opportunities like that for him for a while, once he was flying solo. And she wouldn't have many more opportunities with the kids herself. As trying as her experiences with them had been at times, Poppy was going to miss Quinn and Finn after she returned to Boston. She was going to miss Chance, too.

"Usually, when the guys come over," he said as she descended the stairs, "we top off the night with a good rye whiskey. You interested?"

She told herself to say no. Even the single beer

she'd had with dinner had made her sleepy. Despite that, "Sure," she said. "That would be nice."

They took their drinks back outside. As noisy as the mornings were with the birds chattering and woodpeckers banging, the nights in Chance's back-yard were virtually silent. An owl hooted deeply from one of the trees, and a bat was flapping softly around the yard's perimeter, but other than that, there was only the soft murmur of the wind as it rippled through the leaves. Chance sat in the chair nearest her, which was even nearer than usual, close enough that she could reach over and touch him if she wanted to. And she did want to. Very much. She just didn't want to want to.

He smelled like charcoal and whiskey and a sub-urban summer night, a combination Poppy never would have thought she'd find irresistible. As if to ward off the feelings threatening to overwhelm her, she pulled her legs up into the chair in front of her-self, leaned her head back, closed her eyes and en-joyed the peace and quiet. And she wondered how she was ever going to readjust to her evenings in Boston after nights like this.

"What are you thinking about?" she heard Chance ask from what seemed like a million miles away.

When she opened her eyes, though, he was right there beside her, and she had to curb the urge once again to touch him. She didn't want to tell him she'd been wondering how she was ever going to find nights in Boston appealing again, so she responded with what she'd been thinking about upstairs.

"I was thinking about how you and I are the only family Quinn and Finn have left."

He looked puzzled. "But what about your family up in Boston? Your brother and sister are her cousins, too. Your mom and dad are her aunt and uncle."

Poppy was stunned by the reminder. Oh. Right. Her parents and siblings were also related to the children. How weird that she wouldn't have thought to include them in the equation earlier. Even so, her family's ties to Adele were essentially limited to blood alone. And the other members of her family would have just as soon not acknowledged even that.

"Although that's true," she said, "I was the only member of my family who was ever really close to Adele and her family when we were growing up."

"Why is that?"

She could have just told him it was because the rest of her family was narrow-minded and intolerant, and let it go at that. But Chance's brother had married into Poppy's extended family, and maybe for that reason, if nothing else, he deserved to know the truth about them.

"Adele's mom was my mother's little sister," she

said, "and their family was pretty much the social equivalent of my father's family."

"But?" Chance asked. "I sense a *but* coming. And also a story."

Oh, there was definitely a story to be told. But it didn't exactly end with *and they lived happily-ever-after*. It was going to also necessitate her having to reveal to Chance things about herself and her family she was reluctant to have him know. She didn't know why. Something about mentioning her family's wealth and position just felt out of place in the here and now. Something about mentioning her family at all felt out of place. She didn't want to chill the warmth of Chance's life here in Endicott with the frostiness of her own back in Boston.

In spite of that, she said, "My aunt Georgina, Adele's mom, married *way* beneath her social station, and the rest of her family—including my mother— cut her off."

"What do you mean they *cut her off*?"

"I mean my grandparents altered their will to exclude her, my great-grandparents revoked the trust funds they'd set up for her when she was born—so did Aunt Georgina's other grandparents—and my mother stopped speaking to her. Everyone in the family stopped speaking to her, actually."

"People actually do that?" Chance asked. "Just

start pretending someone they love doesn't exist anymore?"

"They do where I come from," Poppy told him. Probably because her family's concept of love didn't correspond to his own family's concept of love.

"Jeez, just how far beneath her station did she marry?" he asked.

She could tell from his expression that he found the idea of cutting someone off for doing something like that pretty stupid. Which, of course, it was.

"My uncle Joaquín was a mechanic," Poppy told him. "He worked for the public school system, keeping the buses running."

"That's super important work," Chance said. "You can't have kids riding in dangerous vehicles."

"I agree. And he was the kindest man I ever met." Somehow, she was able to stop herself before finishing that sentence with *until now*. "And Aunt Georgina loved him like nobody's business. But the rest of the family did not approve of him. At all. They were scandalized that she even wanted to associate with someone like him, never mind get married and start a family."

"We can't help who we fall in love with."

"No, we can't," Poppy agreed. "But there are still a lot of people in the world—in the world I come from, anyway—who think it's more important to stay true to your roots than to stay true to a perfectly lovely person who doesn't come from the same root system."

"So then how did you and Adele get so close?"

"She and I ended up in the same ballet class when I was in kindergarten. I think Aunt Georgina enrolled her specifically so she'd have an excuse to see my mother at practices and try to smooth things over with her and, ultimately, the rest of the family."

"Did it work?"

"Not for my mother and Aunt Georgina. My mother refused to make amends. But Adele and I became great friends. As much as my mother disliked me seeing her, she didn't have much choice but to let me, because I threw such a fit when she tried to take me out of ballet class. And when we were older, I only lived a couple of miles away from Adele. Close enough that I could ride my bike to her house after school."

Maintaining her friendship with her cousin was the only time in her life that Poppy ever stood up to her mother. Because Adele was the only real friend Poppy ever had. All the other children she'd socialized with as a kid had been handpicked by her parents. And she hadn't liked any of them any more than they'd liked her. But Adele... Adele had understood what it was like to be an outcast and a disappointment within her own family because of her mother's situation. And she wasn't afraid to show affection to those she loved. Poppy had adored her cousin for that.

"So...your folks are, like, stupid rich, huh?" Chance asked.

There was no point in denying it anymore. Not that she'd ever denied it to him. She just hadn't exactly been forthcoming. "Yeah," she said. "They're stupid rich." *In more ways than one*, she couldn't help thinking.

"I mean, I figured you guys were pretty well-off from all the high-powered attorney stuff you mentioned last night and your great-aunt Theodora being such a black sheep, but... But it sounds like your family is really, really, *really* rich."

Poppy sighed her resignation. "The Digbys are one of the most prominent families in Boston and have been for a couple of centuries. My father and mother both wield a lot of power there. And in a lot of other places, too."

"Wow."

"It's not as impressive as it sounds."

"Oh, it's exactly as impressive as it sounds."

She wanted to deny it again, but one look at Chance told her it would be pointless.

"What would your parents think about me?" he asked.

Certain she'd only imagined the question in her head, because it sounded like something a man would only ask a woman he was romantically interested in, and Chance couldn't possibly be romantically interested in her, she said, "What?"

"If you and I were dating," he said, "what would your parents think about that?"

Instead of answering him, she said, "We're not dating." And she was surprised at the depth of her disappointment to admit that. It was ridiculous. Poppy didn't want to date anyone. She didn't have time to date anyone. Her life was her job, not another human being. So why did it matter if she dated—or didn't date—anyone? Especially someone she'd only be seeing for a few more days. There would be a thousand miles separating them once she went back to Boston. And beyond the geographic distance, the two of them couldn't be more unsuited. No amount of wishing they were would change any of that.

"But what if we were dating?" Chance insisted. "How would your parents feel? When it comes to social stations, I'm right there next to the school-bus mechanic."

Actually, that wasn't quite true, at least where her parents were concerned. Delilah and Edgar Digby had no use for a bus mechanic in the public school system. They would, however, have use for a man with a boatyard from time to time, since both their sailboat and their yacht needed regular maintenance. That put Chance a full step, possibly even two, above the basement of blue collar. And, hey, he was now the overseer of their extremely wealthy niece and nephew, whose previous insignificance disappeared the minute they came into money. Might be worth buttering him up for that. As a prospective suitor for their daughter, however? Even a daughter who'd spent her life disappointing them?

When she still didn't reply, he said, "They wouldn't approve of me, would they?"

Poppy made herself be honest. "No. They wouldn't."

"Would they cut you off if you married someone like me?"

Again, she sidestepped the question. "I'm not marrying anyone."

He smiled knowingly—and not a little resentfully—at her refusal to answer. "They would, wouldn't they?"

She sighed again. "Honestly? I don't know. Times have changed, some, even in the world where I grew up. I mean, my brother, Barnaby, is married to a woman whose father owns a hardware store."

That seemed to hearten him for some reason. "Seriously?"

"Well, okay, it's a national chain of home improvement stores that he inherited from his father, but still."

Now Chance looked deflated. "That's three generations of wealth there, Poppy," he pointed out.

"Three generations of wealth is *very* nouveau riche to my folks. And nouveau riche isn't exactly de rigueur for them. You should have seen my mother's face when my sister-in-law said they were having their wedding reception at the New England Aquarium."

"That'd be a cool place to have a reception."

"Mother thought it was too showy," Poppy told him.

"Is your sister married?"

"No, but Odette is engaged to a hedge fund manager." She sighed before adding the rest. "Whose father is an Italian marquis and whose mother comes from a Swiss banking family."

Chance nodded knowingly at that. "So safe to say a guy like me isn't going to be invited to your folks' house for dinner anytime soon."

"Probably not."

"And there's a good chance you'd lose everything if you married a guy like me."

"Yes," she told him. "There is a chance of that. Not that I care," she hastened to add. "It doesn't matter to me if I'm ever cut out of my parents' will or have my trust funds revoked by my grandparents. I can make my own way in the world." Not to mention there were some things that were a lot more important than money. But Chance surely knew that, so it went without saying.

"But they'd stop speaking to you, too," he said.

"They'd never welcome you back to the home you grew up in."

That was probably true. But all she said was "It's possible. As I said, though, I'm not marrying anyone."

"Yeah, you did say that," Chance conceded. "A couple of times."

"My job is much too important to me," she assured him. Even if, for some reason, she was beginning to feel not quite as sure about that as she once was. "And I don't have time as it is for a relationship."

"Yeah, you've mentioned that, too."

"And after my promotion, I'll have even less time."

"So you're good, then."

"I'm good."

Funny, though, how neither of them seemed to believe that. And funny how she didn't feel very good about that at all.

Chapter Nine

Tuesday morning started the same way Monday morning had, with Poppy's alarm going off before dawn, her pilfering of a shirt from Chance's closet and her grabbing her tablet from the nightstand to head downstairs, popping her head in to check on the kids on her way. That, however, was where the repetition ended, because only Quinn was in her sleeping bag. Finn's was empty. Pippi was gone, too.

He must have taken her out for her morning, ah, constitutional, Poppy thought, battling back a twinge of alarm. After checking Chance's office and the upstairs bathroom—both were empty—she hurried downstairs and out the back door. But the backyard was empty, too. She spun around and sped through the house to the front door, disengaging the chain and dead bolt to throw it open, and ran into the front yard. But it, too, was vacant.

"Finn!" she called as loudly as she could. "Finn, are you out here?"

Her only reply was a bird whose call seemed to say, *He gone, he gone, he gone.*

"Tell me something I don't know," she muttered back.

She called out for the boy a few more times, but he never answered. The twinge of alarm she'd been feeling was turning to full-blown panic as she went back into the house. Her actions must have woken Chance, because he was standing in the living room, tugging a T-shirt over his head, when she got back inside. He still looked groggy from sleep, but when he saw her state, he roused quickly.

"What's wrong?" he asked.

"Finn's not in his room," she told him.

That woke him up completely. "He must have taken Pippi out."

She shook her head. "I already checked. He's not outside."

"Then he must be in the house somewhere."

They made a quick search of the first floor, checking every room, opening every closet, every cabinet, every cupboard. Then they headed down into the basement and scoured every inch. The garage, too, offered no sign of him. Finn was nowhere. By the time Poppy met up again with Chance in the kitchen, her panic was off the charts. She told herself little boys were excellent at hiding and that Finn was even more precocious and rambunctious than most. He was exactly the type of child who would want to prank his keepers. But puppies were less successful when it came to secreting themselves away. The fact that Pippi wasn't yipping senselessly made things even scarier.

"He's not here anywhere," Poppy said.

"I'm sure he's fine," Chance told her. But he looked just as worried as she was. "He has to be upstairs, then, hiding somewhere. You know how those kids are. He just wants to give us a hard time."

"I don't think so," she said. "Pippi must be with him, and she's not making a sound. Something's off."

They hurried back upstairs and gave that level just as thorough a check as the others. Finn was nowhere upstairs, either. They returned to the children's room to find Quinn still sound asleep, in spite of their less-than-quiet efforts to find her brother. If Finn took off, she would have slept right through it. Despite that, Poppy shook her gently to wake her.

"Quinn," she said softly. "Honey. Wake up. Do you know where Finn is?"

Quinn rubbed her eyes and sat up in her sleeping bag. Her hair was sticking up, and her face was imprinted with the folds of her pillow. Poppy gave her a minute to orient herself, even though every minute that passed only compounded her fear.

"Sweetie?" she said in an effort to move Quinn along. "Do you know where your brother is?"

She shook her head.

Chance settled on his haunches beside her. "Do you know where he might have gone? Did he say anything last night before you guys went to sleep?"

Quinn shook her head again. "But he had a dream about Mommy and Daddy last night," she said. "I woke up to pee, and he was crying."

"Did he tell you what the dream was about?"

This time, Quinn nodded. "He said Mommy and Daddy were in a big forest, and they were planting trees."

The color drained from Chance's face. "A forest?"

Quinn nodded again. "He said he wanted to help them, but when he got close to where they were, they moved to a different place. And then, when he got close to where they were again, they moved somewhere else. Every time he got close to them, they moved, and he couldn't get to them. It made him really sad." Tears suddenly filled her eyes. "It made me sad, too."

Chance looked at Poppy. "The woods," he said. "Finn is out in the nature preserve with Pippi, looking for his parents."

Now the color drained from Poppy's face, too. "Oh, no."

"Uncle Chance?" Quinn said. "Is Finn okay?"

"He'll be fine, sweetheart," he told her. And Poppy hoped Quinn was young enough that she couldn't detect the very obvious fear in his voice. "Go back to sleep, if you can," he added. "Poppy and I have to make a phone call."

The two of them headed out of the room with Quinn trailing not far behind. "He'll be okay," he repeated as he headed back down the stairs. "There's nothing dangerous in the woods—"

"Oh, except *coyotes*," Poppy reminded him. She kept her voice low, though, so as not to scare Quinn.

"They won't bother people," he insisted just as softly.

"No, but they might go after a little puppy that's following a little boy. And if that little boy gets in the way…"

It didn't bear thinking about. So she pushed the thought away.

"He'll be fine," Chance repeated. "The woods are safe. There aren't any marked trails, though, and he could get lost."

"Are there cliffs?" Poppy asked. "Are there

creeks? Are there dangerous things to trip over and hit heads on?"

Chance didn't respond to that. Not that his silence didn't tell her all she needed to know. A six-year-old boy who had little to no experience hiking in the woods was out hiking in the woods. Alone. That wasn't safe. Period.

"How big is the nature preserve?" she asked.

He hesitated. "About two hundred acres."

That was a lot of space to lose a child. And it provided a lot of ways for him to get hurt.

"Look, if he keeps walking in a straight line," Chance said, "he'll end up on the other side at the visitor's center or in someone's backyard. And there's a fire road that crosses in the other direction. If he wanders onto that and follows it far enough, he'll be able to find his way to one of the highways."

"There are *highways*?" Poppy fairly shouted. "Are you telling me he could get hit by a *truck*?"

"They're both two-lane state roads that hardly ever get used," Chance assured her. Somehow, though, Poppy wasn't reassured at all.

"Poppy?" Quinn interjected plaintively. "Uncle Chance? Is Finn okay?"

"He'll be fine, sweetheart," Chance assured her.

"And if he doesn't find the fire road?" Poppy asked. "If he doesn't make his way straight across to the other side? If he only wanders in circles for hours?"

Chance grabbed his phone from the coffee table and hit 911. And as he waited for a dispatcher to answer, he repeated, like a mantra, "He'll be fine."

By noon, there were scores of people scouring the nature preserve for Finn and Pippi. Not just folks from the police and fire departments, but Felix and Max and a handful of Chance's other acquaintances. As word got out about the missing boy, more people, many total strangers, showed up to help search. He'd always known his hometown was the kind of place that pulled together in a crunch, but even he was amazed at the depth of the concern for a little boy who, a few days ago, hadn't even been a part of their community. And he was grateful to every single person who was currently in the woods with him and Poppy trying to find him.

Save Finn's disappearance, it was another gorgeous day, the sky cloudless and clear, the temperature hovering in the low seventies. As soon as Chance had hung up the phone after calling 911, he'd changed into shorts, a T-shirt and hiking boots, and after telling Poppy to wait for the cops to show up and give them the details, he'd headed into the woods himself. Quinn hadn't been able to tell them what time it was when Finn had had his nightmare, but even with a head start of hours, Chance figured the boy couldn't have gotten that far. The woods weren't terribly overgrown, but they could be challenging, especially for a child.

Even though, as he'd told Poppy, there were no marked trails, there were a handful that existed simply because people liked to go into the woods. They generally entered in a handful of different places and headed the same way, something that had created de facto trails over the years. Chance had discovered shortly after moving into his house that one of those trails ran right behind his yard. Once Finn made it a couple dozen feet into the woods, he would have found it. Chance had figured when he first entered the woods that morning that it made sense to follow that trail first. Until he remembered it must have been full dark when Finn made his way into the woods. He might not have seen the trail at all. That was when he realized, oh, hell, the kid could be anywhere.

That fact was still abundantly clear hours later, when he and Poppy, who had joined him during one of his brief returns to the house, breached the trees and emerged onto the fire road just after noon. It had been six hours since they discovered Finn was missing. And no one had seen a single sign of him.

He checked his phone for updates, but there were none. The last text had come from one of the local

Eagle Scouts who were helping out, who'd found a fruit snack wrapper he thought might have belonged to Finn. But Poppy and Chance had known better. Not only did Finn not like fruit snacks, Chance hadn't bought any he could have taken from the house. So onward went the search.

"Maybe he's not in the woods," Poppy said as she drew up beside Chance. "Maybe he went somewhere else."

In spite of the mild temperatures, she was, like Chance, damp with sweat. And also streaked with grime and littered with the detritus of the woods— bits of leaves and twigs were nestled in her hair and clinging to her sleeveless white shirt and beige shorts. She'd had to come out here in her sandals, though, because she hadn't had any footwear appropriate for walking. He'd noticed her limping for the past hour, but she hadn't complained once.

"I don't know where else he could be," Chance told her.

Even though that wasn't quite true. Over the course of the morning, a number of possible scenarios for Finn's whereabouts had unfolded in his brain. For one thing, if he *had* taken Pippi out for her morning relief, it was possible he had been snatched out of the yard by a stranger or one of Chance's neighbors. And although that was *extremely* unlikely, it was still possible. It was also possible Finn had fallen into a storm drain and been swept away by runoff. Which was also *extremely* unlikely, because they hadn't had any rain for more than a week. And it was possible Finn had eaten poisonous mushrooms and was sick somewhere in the woods. Again, unlikely, since Chance had spent a lot of time in the nature preserve and had never seen any poisonous ingestible plants growing anywhere.

And then there were the other prospects—also unlikely, but still possible—inevitably unfolding in his head. That Finn had encountered bears. Or wolves. Or fae folk. Or a troupe of traveling circus performers who'd convinced him to join them and become a trapeze artist.

Oh, Chance was just scratching the surface of all the many, *many* things that could happen to an unsupervised—and even supervised—child. He had learned fast today just how much of his life now was going to involve staving off the borderline terror that something awful could happen to his nephew or niece—or both—and that he was going to have to live with that terror *forever*.

"It's never going to go away, is it?" he said softly.

"What?" Poppy asked.

"The fear. Those kids… They're so small. So helpless. They have no idea how to take care of themselves. That's all on me. And that's never going to stop scaring me, is it?"

Strangely, she seemed to understand. She placed a tentative hand on his arm and, after a small hesitation, gave it a single stroke. It was an awkward touch, as if she weren't used to comforting people. But it was comforting nonetheless.

"No, I don't imagine it will," she told him.

"I mean, even if they're not lost in the woods, there are so many other things that can happen to them. And they can happen at a moment's notice, with no preparation. Broken bones. Illness. Predators. Bullies. Random acts of violence. Being in the wrong place at the wrong time and then just…"

As the fears bombarded him again, he started to feel sick, and he punctuated the statement with a strangled sound. It was only because Poppy gave his arm a gentle squeeze that he was able to bring himself back from the brink. Barely.

She'd been doing a lot of that today, he realized now—brushing her palm lightly over his back or giving his hand a soft graze whenever he voiced his concerns for Finn. Only now was it hitting him how much those gestures had kept him from going over the brink and into the abyss of stark-raving panic. He wouldn't have thought such simple touches from someone could have such a major impact. But from Poppy, they totally did.

Without thinking, he covered her hand with his. When he did, her eyes flew to his, her gaze looking a little panicky, too. For a moment, he thought she would jerk her hand back. Instead, she curled her fingers softly into his flesh again. And, again, Chance felt some of the tension ease out of him.

"You can't let thoughts like that overwhelm you," she told him. "Yes, those are all things that can happen, but statistically speaking, they won't."

"Tell that to the irrational side of my brain," he said.

She smiled. "The irrational side will eventually learn to cope," she told him. "Because the rational side will step in. There are a lot of wonderful things that you'll be able to focus on instead of all the things that can go wrong. And they're things that will definitely happen. There will be school plays. Birthday parties. Christmas mornings. Even the mundane stuff like reading them your favorite books or making dinner together or going out on the boat or watching them chasing around the yard with Pippi."

He did his best to smile back. And even if the gesture didn't quite hit the mark, he was grateful to her for reminding him there could be—would be—more to life than fear. And he found himself wishing she would be there with him to share in the very times she described.

"You have so many memories to make with these children, Chance," she continued. "So many fun times to have with them. And as those good things happen, they're going to crowd into your head, and they're going to take the place of the fears."

"How do you know this stuff?" he asked. Some icy, ruthless cutthroat she was turning out to be.

She sighed. "I guess it was something I had to learn myself after the twins were born. Adele and Logan experienced the same anxiety with Quinn and Finn when they were babies that you're experiencing now. To a lesser degree, I did, too. Because I loved those kids, too. I still love them. And as… challenging…as the last week has been with them, there have been some good times, too. Like yesterday. Focus on how much fun you had with the kids yesterday and how many more days like that you have ahead of you. Don't think about the fear."

Easier said than done, he thought. But he made himself do what she said. He thought about the day before, about the children's fascination with all the tools and machines in his shop and their laughter as he tossed them into the river. He thought about their joy when they realized they were Pippi's new owners. About the barrage of questions they asked about, well, everything. Poppy was right. They could be challenging. But they'd also made him laugh and look at the world a little differently. And they'd made him feel things he hadn't felt in a long time. Things he'd never thought he would feel again.

Then again, it wasn't only the kids who'd been making him feel those things, he realized. Poppy had been a big part of the last couple of days, too.

He threw his head back and looked up at the sky. It was the same one that had been overhead his entire life. So why did he feel like he was in an entirely new place today?

"How did everything change so quickly?" he wondered.

He didn't realize he had spoken the question aloud until Poppy replied, "I think it's probably because you've already started loving your niece and nephew."

He snapped his head back to look at her. *Can that really be it?* he asked himself. Could just a couple of days with the kids have already caused such a reaction in him? Could he really love a couple of total strangers?

Then he remembered how much Finn and Quinn had reminded him of his brother, right from the start. He recalled the memories of his father that had washed over him when he was in the train store with Finn. He remembered how Quinn always sat in her chair the same way his mother had, with one ankle tucked under her knee and her head resting in her hand with part of her mouth covered. And he realized they weren't strangers at all. His entire family was in those kids. Of course he would love them. Right from the start. They were his family. And they would be with him forever. And if what he felt for the kids after a few days was love, then did that mean what he was feeling for Poppy was…?

He pushed that last thought away before it could form. Mostly. "Guess it's easier to love someone than I thought," he said. And why that surprised him so much, he had no idea. It should be easy to love someone. Loving should come as naturally as breathing.

He didn't realize he'd said that out loud, either, until Poppy replied softly, "Sometimes it does."

It was a cryptic response. He was about to ask her what she meant, but his phone pinged with a message, and he nearly dropped it trying to read what it said. He expelled a breath of relief and a sound of gratitude.

"They found him," he told her. "Felix and Max found him and Pippi by the frog pond. They're taking him back to the house now."

After a long afternoon of thanking seemingly a million people a million times—and buying them all lunch with a massive to-go delivery from Pandora's Pita Palazzo—Chance felt a little more stable. He and Poppy had talked to both kids about never *ever* going off anywhere on their own, and to always, *always* find Chance first to tell him where they wanted or needed to go. He, in turn, had promised he would be available to them no matter what and would somehow make sure they were able to do whatever they needed to do, as soon as they could, provided it was safe for all of them.

He also promised to take them into the nature preserve to explore on a regular basis, and he challenged them to help him figure out a way to mark a trail from the backyard to the other side in a way that wouldn't harm the woods, building rock piles or arranging sticks on the ground, tying strings on branches, that kind of thing. It would be their first adventure together, he told them. The first of many to come.

Now, as he and Poppy sat on the patio, watching the sun dip low toward the trees as the kids and Pippi scampered around the yard, he unscrewed the top off a much-needed pale ale while she sipped a glass of much-needed wine. And he realized it was going to be a long time before he was able to take his eyes off Finn and Quinn. His family.

"Hell of a day," he said after his first sip.

"Hell of a day," she agreed. "Tomorrow will be better."

"It better be."

They both chuckled at that. Then a comfortable

silence settled. It was the third night in a row that he and Poppy had enjoyed on his patio, and he realized he was beginning to like that a lot. He'd liked finding her out here yesterday morning, too, working in one of his shirts, as if it were the most normal thing in the world for her to do. This time last week, Chance had spent every waking moment at his house alone. And he had liked that a lot, too. He'd always considered himself a pretty solitary creature. Now he was beginning to wonder.

The children came running up to them, Pippi yelping behind them, and both kids climbed into the third Adirondack chair together. Before either Chance or Poppy could say a word, Finn broke the silence.

"Uncle Chance, what happens when people die?"

Chance wasn't exactly surprised by the question. But neither did he know how to answer it. He remembered Poppy telling him to be honest with the kids when they talked about their parents. So he made himself be honest.

"I don't know, Finn," he said. "Some people think when you die, you go to a place called Heaven, where everything is perfect, and everyone is happy, and you get to spend forever with all the people you love. Some people think that, after you die, you come back to life again as someone else."

Finn smiled at that. "Like Mommy and Daddy could be somebody's babies right now?"

Chance shrugged. "Yeah, maybe. Other people think that, after you die, the stuff that made you alive all sort of mixes together with the stuff that makes everything else alive—other people and animals and plants and everything that's ever been alive—and all that mixed-together stuff goes to make more people and animals and plants and everything that's alive."

Finn eyed him intently. "So, like, trees and rabbits and people all have the same stuff? Stuff that used to be in other trees and rabbits and people?"

"Yeah. Kind of like that," Chance told him. "And then there are some people who think that, after you die, there's nothing, and you stop being or feeling anything at all. But some people find comfort in that."

Finn thought about everything Chance had said. "I don't think there's nothing," he decided.

"I don't think there's nothing, either," Chance agreed. He just didn't know exactly what there was. Maybe he and Finn could work it out together someday.

"Uncle Chance, can we plant some trees in the backyard for Mommy and Daddy?" the boy asked.

Chance looked over at Poppy when Finn said that. She'd been watching the two of them intently, he could see. But Finn's simple question had brought tears to her eyes.

"Yeah, Finn," he said, "we can plant some trees for your mom and dad. And every spring, when their leaves start showing up, you can think how maybe that's your mom and dad, checking up on you. And when they're big enough to make shade, you can think maybe it's them still protecting you. The same way they would if they were here."

Finn smiled at that, and something inside Chance smiled a little bit, too. It really had been one hell of a day. But it had ended well. And for the first time in a long time, he realized he couldn't wait to see what the next day held.

Then he remembered that no matter what it held, Poppy would be here with him. Which made him look forward to the day even more.

Chapter Ten

The children's furniture and other belongings arrived on Wednesday, a day ahead of schedule.

Poppy was on the patio working when she received the call from the moving company, telling her the truck was en route and would arrive before noon. She told herself she should be delighted. She'd promised the children she would stay long enough to get them unpacked and settled, which shouldn't take more than the rest of the day. That meant she could return to Boston tomorrow. She could go back to work at the office. Back to all the resources she needed to prepare for her upcoming trial. Back to her apartment. To her routine. To all the things that were familiar to her. To all the things that were important. She could go back to her normal life. Back to being her usual self.

If only she could remember what that was. Because at some point over her short stay in Endicott, Poppy had started to lose a part of herself to this sweet and gentle place. And, she had to admit, to the sweet and gentle man who lived here. Instead of feeling delighted about her return to Boston, she was distressed by the realization that she was marking her last hours here and might never come back. It would make more sense for Chance to bring the children to Boston for visits, since that would allow them to see their friends and reconnect with their favorite places there. She found some small comfort that she would still see Chance from time to time, but it would be in a city that felt alien to her now—for a lot of reasons. There would be little, if any, opportunity or reason for her to return to Endicott and spend time with him and the children here. And for some reason, that bothered Poppy a lot.

"I thought you said the movers wouldn't be here until tomorrow," Chance said as the truck pulled up in front of his house a few hours later.

"No, I said by tomorrow at the latest," she reminded him. Though she was no happier to see them here early than he clearly was.

He looked at her questioningly. "You told the kids you'd stay until their things arrived from Boston."

"Yes," she said. She wasn't sure what else to say. So she said nothing more.

Chance didn't seem to know what to say, either. But after a moment, he added, "You said you'd help them get everything unpacked and situated."

"Yes."

He hesitated again. "But I'm guessing they don't have that much stuff to unpack."

"No. They don't."

He looked as if there were a million things going through his head that he wanted to say. There were a million things going through her head that she wanted to say, too. She just wasn't sure how. She'd never felt the way she was feeling now—as if she were about to lose the most important thing in the world.

His gaze locked with hers so intently it was impossible for her to look away. But all he said was "It probably won't take more than an afternoon to get them settled."

This time Poppy was the one to hesitate. "No. It probably won't."

He nodded with the sort of resolution one might

show when told a situation was hopeless. "Guess that means you'll be leaving in the next day or two."

She knew she couldn't stay any longer than she'd promised. Though now, she realized, it wasn't only because she needed to get back to Boston to prepare for her trial. It was also because every extra moment she spent with Chance and the children would only make it that much harder to leave.

"Tomorrow," she told him. "I'll have to go back to Boston tomorrow."

"That soon?"

She nodded.

"But you'll miss Bob," he told her.

She remembered he'd said the comet would make its closest pass to the planet on Thursday night, and that that was when it…he…whatever…was at the peak of its/his magic. But the fact that she would be missing such an enchanting moment seemed fitting somehow. Something told her she would be missing a lot of enchanting moments in her life from here on out. And the realization that she had become the kind of woman who thought in terms of enchanting moments only made it that much more imperative that she leave Endicott. She wasn't a woman of enchanting moments. She was an icy, ruthless, cutthroat attorney. One who never lost a case. She couldn't afford to forget that.

"I'm sorry," she told him.

He nodded again, even more helplessly. "Yeah," he said. "Yeah, I bet."

"Chance—"

But he was turning away to meet the movers at the front door, and after that, conversation that didn't center on the children's possessions was impossible.

The movers made short work of expelling from their truck every physical thing the children had left to their names and depositing it all into the two now-vacant bedrooms upstairs—Chance had asked Felix and Max to help him move what was left of his office furniture to the basement the night before. By the time the movers were headed off to their next destination, all remnants of Chance and Poppy's earlier conversation had completely evaporated. They and the kids were left to stand in the hallway between both rooms, looking into each to see literal piles of furniture, boxes and bags scattered about and having no idea where to start.

"Sooo," Chance began, stringing the single syllable out over several time zones, "why don't I just leave you and the kids to sort all this out?"

"Me?" Poppy said. "Why me? It's your house. You should be the one in charge."

"But it's the kids' rooms," he countered. "I've never decorated a kid's room in my life. Logan and I always shared a room, and him being older, he always got to make the decisions on what went where. I mean, I picked the spots over my bed to hang my Linkin Park poster and my Junior Boater Award, but that was about it."

"I've never decorated a kid's room, either," Poppy assured him.

"Oh, right," he said. "Older sister. I forgot. Guess you and she had the same arrangement."

Poppy almost laughed at that. The town house in Beacon Hill where she grew up had claimed four floors and eight thousand square feet. There had been days when she didn't even see her sister or brother.

"No, I had my own room," she told him. "But my mother always had a decorator come in to do the whole house, including our rooms, when we were kids."

"A decorator for a kid's room?" Chance echoed. "Seriously?"

"She liked for our house to have a theme," Poppy explained. "And she liked to switch out the theme every couple of years."

"Sounds expensive," he said. "But I guess when you're one of the wealthiest, most powerful families in town, that's the way you roll."

There was no rancor in his voice, no criticism or condemnation. There was only a matter-of-factness that reiterated the massive social chasm that separated them and how difficult it would be for the two of them to effectively span it.

Poppy said nothing. She didn't know why it bothered her for Chance to know how well-off her family was. It wasn't like it was her money. But standing here, in his modest but charming house, surrounded by his unassuming but homey effects, and realizing how much different it was from the environment in which she'd grown up—and how different it was from the world to which she'd be returning—she just felt…odd. She told herself there was nothing wrong with being from wealth. And there wasn't. The twins' parents had probably been on a financial par with her own, and they were perfectly normal, for the most part. So why did Poppy suddenly feel so uncomfortable about her own upbringing? She was normal, too. For the most part.

This was a stupid conversation to be having with her brain. She made herself think of something else instead. Like how good Chance looked today in a different pair of battered khaki shorts and a different camp shirt, this one mottled with tiny cartoon cocktails. His dark hair was shoved back from his face with careless fingers, something that only made his smoky gray eyes look even more smoldering.

"But what if you didn't like the theme she chose?" he asked.

"Oh, I always liked the themes she chose," Poppy assured him.

He looked like he didn't believe her.

"I did," she insisted. "My bedroom never looked better than when I was nine, during her Tuscany phase, when it had the terra-cotta walls and travertine tile floor. And the oil paintings of the vineyards were divine." And, hey, even if the floor had been cold as ice every time she got up to go to the bathroom, and even if the rows of grapevines in the paintings had looked like terrifying snakes when the lights were off, that was a small price to pay for such an exquisite room. Wasn't it?

Chance still didn't look convinced. "Mmm. Not many nine-year-olds would go for oil paintings and travertine tile."

"Well, I sure did," Poppy contended. "It was almost as nice as when I was five and she did the English-cottage thing. Chintz chairs and botanical prints and a Staffordshire lamp I wasn't allowed to touch. It was amazing."

"Yeah, that sounds like every five-year-old's dream room all right."

"Anyway," Poppy said, "I think we should both help the children put everything together."

"Can we paint my room purple?" Quinn asked. "My room in Boston was purple."

Chance looked vaguely horrified by the question. But he replied, "Um, sure, Quinn. Any color you want."

"My walls were like a chalkboard," Finn added. "So I could draw on them. Can I do that here?"

Chance's horror seemed to compound. "Like a black chalkboard?"

"Yeah."

"The whole room?"

"Uh-huh."

"Someone actually invented a paint for that?"

Finn nodded earnestly, looking fearful his uncle was going to tell him no.

"I…uh… Okay," Chance said. "We can do that, too. Just…not today, okay? First things first."

"Okay," the children chorused somberly.

"Soon, though," he told them. "I promise."

They nodded as one, and their tension seemed to ease some. Although Poppy figured they were happy to finally have all their stuff here in Endicott, *all their stuff* now was a fraction of what it had been before their move. They'd had such large quarters in their old house that it would have been impossible for them to fit everything into their much smaller rooms here.

"So where do we start?" Chance asked.

Poppy looked into first one bedroom, then the other. The messes were equally chaotic. "Pick a room," she said. "And start unpacking."

* * *

After flipping a coin, they started in Finn's room, organizing the boy's belongings with surprising efficiency. After reassembling his twin bed and covering it with Avengers sheets and bedspread, they pushed his sole dresser into a corner and filled it and the closet with his clothes. Clothes, Chance couldn't help noticing, that looked a lot like his own, save their much smaller size—something that made him wonder if maybe he should do something about his own wardrobe. It didn't help when he looked down and realized he was wearing one of his many grilling shirts today. Which was a lot like his many boating shirts and his many hiking shirts. He should probably have at least a few pieces in his closet that didn't scream *Failure to Launch*. Especially now that he had someone like Poppy in his life, who, he was sure, was normally surrounded by men who didn't dress like a six-year-old.

He reminded himself that he didn't have Poppy in his life. At least, not in any way that it mattered what kind of clothes he owned. And it bothered him how much he disliked that realization. It bothered him even more how much he disliked the realization that she had men in her life back in Boston who didn't dress like a six-year-old. Even if she didn't have a serious partner, she must see guys every day in her work and social circles who looked like they just stepped out of the pages of *GQ*. That realization bothered Chance, too.

Not that *any* of it mattered, he reminded himself, because she would be leaving tomorrow. Sure, they'd still be in contact after that, but she wouldn't be physically around. Why that bothered him so much, he couldn't say. It wasn't like the two of them were soul mates. They didn't even have anything in common. Their upbringings and visions of the future couldn't have been more different. Their values and dispositions were totally at odds. There was absolutely nothing that connected them, save a tie to two children who needed them. Hell, they'd only met a few days ago.

So why did it feel like they were super connected? Why did it seem like they'd known each other for years? And why, dammit, did he hate so much the thought of her going back to her life in Boston?

He looked at her now, on the other side of the room, where she and Quinn were lining up action figures on top of a bookcase. Even in her casual clothes, she looked completely out of his league. She sure was cute, though, in her cropped pale green pants and sleeveless white shirt. He'd never really gone for women with short hair—or brunettes, for that matter—but the style had a lot to recommend it. Not the least of which was how it showed off an incredibly sexy neck he found himself wanting to drag his open mouth along until he hit the delicate, surprisingly erotic, pearls encircling her neck. Then past them to the open collar of her shirt. Then to the first button, which he would immediately unfasten, so that he could move even lower, tasting the rosy skin between her breasts. Then pushing aside her bra to trace his tongue along the lower curve of first one breast, then the other. Then even lower, opening her shirt wider, button by button, until he could skim it off her completely and lay her on her back and—

And *holy hell*, what was he *thinking*? In front of six-year-olds? What was wrong with him?

Naturally, Poppy chose that moment to look up at him, and the carefree smile on her lips immediately disappeared to be replaced by a surprised—and unbelievably arousing—*o*. Her eyes darkened, her cheeks grew stained with pink and he realized without a doubt that she knew exactly what he'd been thinking about. What he was still thinking about, because no matter how hard he tried, he couldn't shove the idea of…tasting her…out of his brain. Except now it was obvious that she was thinking about it, too, and she didn't seem to be too put off by the idea. In fact, she seemed to be thinking about dragging her open mouth along some of his body parts, and—

And *holy hell*, what was he *thinking* again? What was *she* thinking? And more to the point, what were they going to do about it?

"Hey, could I talk to you for a minute?" he asked her impulsively. He had no idea why he needed to talk to her for a minute or what he could possibly have to say. What he wanted to say and do would take a lot longer than a minute.

Poppy looked panicked at the question. "Now?"

He nodded. He hoped not too eagerly. "Yeah. It'll just take a minute."

"I… Okay."

He looked at the twins. "You guys will be okay for a minute, right?"

The twins were both too caught up in their activities to even notice the grown-ups were there. "Sure," they said in unified distraction.

"We'll be right back," he assured them.

Poppy rose from the floor just as Chance made his way to the door and followed him out. He didn't even know where he was going. He just knew he needed to put as much distance between them and the kids as possible, so he headed downstairs with Poppy on his heels. Somehow, he found himself in the laundry room, which was little more than a big closet. But it had a door to close, and that seemed important for some reason, and once Poppy was squeezed inside with him, Chance closed it, moving his body in front of it because there just wasn't room for him to do anything else. She pressed herself against the dryer, with barely a breath of air separating them, and looked at him in confusion.

"Is everything okay?" she said.

How could she ask that question with a straight face? He took a deep breath and released it slowly, but it did nothing to quiet the pounding of his heart. "What just happened upstairs?" he asked.

Now she looked spooked again, her pale green eyes wide, her mouth rounding into that sexy little *o* again. "I...I don't... I don't know what you're talking about," she said, stumbling over the words.

"Oh, I think you do."

The room had been warm when they entered it, but in a matter of seconds, the heat had climbed to near combustible levels.

"No," she insisted, the word coming out soft and breathless. "I don't...um...have any...ah...idea."

Chance wasn't going to back down. The two of them had been dancing around an attraction for days. Why it had decided to come to a head at this moment, he had no clue. But he figured it wasn't going to go away unless they addressed it. Not that he wanted it to go away. On the contrary. He just wasn't sure it was a good idea for either of them to act on it right here, right now.

But what the hell.

"So," he began, "if I, say…you know…kissed you right now, how would you react?"

Her eyes went darker, her cheeks grew pinker, her lips parted wider. "Why would you want to kiss me?"

"I don't know," he lied. "But what if I did?"

"I…"

She never finished whatever she'd planned to say. But her mouth was still open, and Chance wasn't a guy to pass up an opportunity like that. Slowly, so she still had time to stop him if she wanted to, he dipped his head forward. Her gaze locked with his, but she said nothing. He lifted a hand to her face and stroked his curled fingers lightly over her cheek. Her eyes fluttered closed at that, and she expelled a helpless little sound that made something inside him roar to life. He lowered his head more, curling his fingers gently around the back of her neck, lifting his other hand to trace the line of her cheekbone. Poppy sighed again, tilting her head into the touch. So he leaned in one last time and brushed his lips over hers, once, twice, three times, four, before covering her mouth completely with his.

Heat exploded in his belly at the contact, seeping into every pore of his body. Poppy melted into him, threading the fingers of one hand through his hair, curling the others into the front of his shirt to pull him closer. For a long time, they kissed, each trying to take command of the embrace. Then Chance spun them around so that Poppy was the one leaning against the door, and he crowded his body against hers, moving his thigh between her legs and pressing it against the heated heart of her. She gasped at the more intimate contact, and he took advantage to taste her more deeply. Then he curved the fingers of one hand beneath her breast and dragged his thumb across its peak. The fingers in his hair tightened, and she tore her mouth from his.

"Oh," she cried softly against his cheek. "Oh, my god."

Chance recaptured her mouth, kissing her deeply again, and moved his hand to the top button of her shirt. Quickly, he freed it, then moved to the next and unfastened it, too. One by one, he undid each button of the garment until it hung completely open. Then he cupped her lace-covered breast with his hand and palmed her tender flesh. She gasped against his mouth, the fingers in his hair curling tighter. But she didn't recoil, didn't hesitate. Instead, she darted her hand beneath his shirt and skimmed her fingers along the bare skin of his torso, setting little fires everywhere she touched him.

He found the front closure of her bra and unsnapped it, freeing her to touch her more intimately. She was so soft. So warm. The rigid peak of her breast pressed insistently against his palm and, unable to help himself, he ducked his head to taste her there. She inhaled sharply and murmured something incoherent, then dropped her hand to his waist, unbuttoning the top button of his fly and yanking down the zipper. And then she was touching him, too, her fingers pushing slowly along the length of him and back again in rhythm to the movement of his mouth and tongue over her breast.

He didn't know how long they stood like that, caressing each other. He only knew if they did it much longer, he was going to go off like a rocket. So he moved his mouth to hers again and circled her wrist with his fingers to reluctantly return her hand to his chest. He arced one arm over her head against the door and dropped his other hand to her hip. Then he kissed her and kissed her and kissed her. Poppy circled his waist with both arms, splaying her hands open over his back, and kissed him in return, pushing her body into his as if she couldn't get close enough. And then, suddenly, she tore her mouth from his and ducked her head against his chest.

"Stop," she whispered hoarsely. "We have to stop."

He knew she was right. Even so, he asked, "Why?"

Instead of giving him a clear answer, she only told him, "I'm sorry."

He pressed his forehead to the crown of hers. "I'm not," he said.

"That never should have happened," she gasped, still not looking at him.

He chuckled softly. "Oh, I don't think there was any way that *wasn't* going to happen."

Neither said anything for a moment, but neither moved, either.

Finally, quietly, she said, "It's, um, it's been a while for me."

"How much of a while?" he asked, wondering why it mattered. For some reason, though, it did. Which was weird, because it had never mattered with a woman before. It wasn't some misplaced sense of male dominion that made him feel that way. He just needed to know if there was another guy in her life anywhere, at any time, who might still be important to her. Because, suddenly, for some reason, he wanted to be the guy who was important to her.

Instead of being specific, however, she only said, "A long while."

A curl of pleasure unwound inside him. If it had been a long while, then there wasn't anyone back in Boston who might prevent something from happening between the two of them here in Endicott. And Chance really wanted something to happen between the two of them here. He wanted a lot to happen between the two of them. Even if she was leaving tomorrow, he wanted her. Even if it wasn't a good idea, considering the geographic, social and philosophical differences between them, he wanted her. Even if they really weren't a good fit, he wanted her. Even if he was still getting acclimated to his new life with the kids and had no idea what the future held for any of them, he wanted her.

He just wanted her. That was the only thing he *was* sure about at the moment. It was pretty clear she wanted him, too. And realizing that, he heard himself say words to her that he'd never spoken to a woman before.

"Let's get a sitter for the kids tonight."

Her head finally snapped up at that. "What? No," she replied breathlessly. But her tone of voice wasn't nearly as adamant as the words she spoke.

"My friend Max's sister Lilah is a grad student who's been sitting kids for years. She doesn't take any crap from anybody. She'll be great with the kids. Just so you and I can have a little time together alone. Before you have to go back to Boston."

"Chance, it's not a good idea."

"Of course it's not a good idea," he agreed. "So let's get a sitter."

"But… I mean… It's not… We shouldn't…"

She didn't finish a single thought. Chance sympathized. His thoughts at the moment were a mess, too. One thing that was clear, though, was that he and Poppy needed some time together alone, without the kids, to see just what the hell was happening between them.

"I'll take you to La Mariposa. That's Felix's restaurant. You said you wanted to go while you were here. And you're only going to be here for one more night."

When she still didn't reply, he continued, "Come on, Poppy. It's only dinner. Just you and me. No kids. So we can… I don't know. Figure out what's going on with us."

She looked like she still wanted to object. "Only dinner," she stated with much conviction.

"Only dinner," he said. Okay, with a bit less conviction. Still.

She started to lift a hand to his face again, then seemed to realize what she was doing and dropped it back to her side. Chance smiled. Until she unwound her other arm from around his waist, twisted herself so that she could move behind him and took as far a step back as she could to disengage.

"Just dinner," she said again, even more emphatically.

"Just dinner," he promised.

And if something besides dinner happened after

dinner, well... Then that would help them figure out what was going on between them even better than dinner would, right?

Chapter Eleven

The restaurant Poppy entered that evening was as charming and inviting as the rest of Endicott. The walls were all different colors reminiscent of the Caribbean, from pale turquoise to soft yellow to lavender to pink. Artwork filled the place, from bright oil paintings of Cuban street life to vintage cars made of papier-mâché to shelves filled with carved wooden saints. Over all of it, soft acoustic guitar played and a lonely-sounding man sang in Spanish.

Poppy had actually visited Cuba once, with a college friend who'd been so enamored of the Rat Pack, she'd wanted to retrace their every step. She remembered well walking around Old Havana among the retro cars and Art Deco buildings and the splashes of color that were everywhere. Felix had captured his heritage beautifully.

Felix was beautiful, too, she couldn't help thinking as he led them to a table for two in the front window. Where Chance's good looks were earthy and unpretentious, Felix looked as if he'd been wrought by the hands of the gods. He was golden all over, from his hair to his eyes to his skin, as if the sun itself gained its luminescence from him. Even his chef's jacket was dark gold, topping baggy chef pants spattered with tiny green and blue butterflies. The *mariposas* for which the restaurant was named.

"You're in luck," he said as they settled into their seats. "Paella is on the menu tonight."

"Oh, hell, yeah," Chance said with much delight.

He looked adorable this evening, as if he'd struggled hard to dress up as much as possible. She was suddenly grateful that her final spontaneous selection at the vintage shop had been a cute retro shirtwaist dress, midnight blue and dotted with tiny stars and crescent moons. It was absolutely nothing like what she normally wore, and she still wasn't sure how successfully she was pulling it off.

Chance, however, looked completely at ease in charcoal Dockers and a white shirt, both of which had been ironed—if not quite expertly. And he'd even ducked out for a haircut at some point in the afternoon. Poppy had mixed feelings about that. Although the shorter hair showed off his handsome features even better—his cheekbones were even more pronounced than she'd realized, and there was a tiny scar on his left eyebrow she hadn't noticed before—she'd kind of liked his shaggy look. And the feel of his hair brushing over her hand as he'd kissed her that afternoon had made her want to tangle her fingers tighter to make sure he never stopped and—

—and wow, that paella sure did sound good.

"Felix makes his paella the way his *abuela* made paella," Chance said. "Except he throws in a few extra mussels for his closest friends."

"And I make my *sazon* a little different from the way Tita did," Felix added. "The Suarez paella recipe goes all the way back to my several-greats-grandmother in Andalusia. No one's ever messed with it till me." He quickly, deftly made the sign of the cross as he added, "*Dios mio*, I hope Tita didn't hear me say any of that. So should I put in an order for two?"

"Is that what you won the James Beard Award for?" Poppy asked.

"It is," he said proudly. "That and my ceviche."

"You won another one?" Chance asked. "You never mentioned it."

"What can I say, *acere*? I don't want to give you and Max an inferiority complex."

Poppy laughed. "We should get one of each," she told Chance. "Then we can share plates."

He grinned, looking a lot happier about the idea than she would have thought. "Sounds perfect," he said.

"Bueno," Felix said. "I'll send out some wine."

He didn't say what wine he would be sending out, but no way was Poppy going to object. She'd never been to a restaurant where the chef was a personal friend of someone in the party. Even her parents, for all the glittery society they moved in, didn't count an award-winning chef among their cronies.

"What does *acere* mean?" she asked as Felix headed back to the kitchen. "I speak a little Spanish, but I've never heard that."

"Pretty much it just means *friend*," Chance said. "I took Spanish all through school, and I was able to talk to his grandmother just fine whenever I was at their place, but not without her chuckling a time or two whenever I did. Cuban Spanish is a bit different from other Spanish."

"He took care of his grandmother when she was alive?"

"Yeah," Chance said. "The same way she took care of him when he was growing up. The same way she took care of me for a while after Logan took off, for that matter."

"Felix's parents are gone?"

Chance nodded. "His mom left town not long after he was born, and he never knew his dad."

"I hate to hear that. He's a nice guy."

"No worries," Chance said. "He and Marisol were always super close. He doesn't even remember his mother." With a smile, he added, "And he is a nice guy. But if you ever call him that, he'll be offended. He likes to think he's a major bad boy."

The conversation stalled for a moment, because there was little more to say about Felix, which meant she and Chance were going to have to talk about something else. Something like, oh…what they'd said they would talk about at dinner earlier that day—what was happening between the two of them. She tried to tell herself there was nothing happening between the two of them. Then she remembered the laundry room. There was definitely something happening between them. She just wished she knew what.

She told herself it was just physical. It really had been a long time for her, and Chance was an extremely sexy man. Beyond that, he was a kind man. A smart man. A funny man. A man who made her feel good in ways that went beyond the physical. But it was ridiculous for her to think there was any more to it than a simple chemical reaction between the two of them. They had nothing in common and more differences than there were stars in the sky. Anything that might happen between them had to be physical at its core. It would burn out quickly and leave them both feeling spent.

"So, about this afternoon," Chance said, reading her mind. Again.

"Yeah," she said slowly. "About that. I don't think we should read too much into it."

His expression was inscrutable. But all he said was "And why is that?"

There were way too many answers to that question. The one Poppy finally settled on was "Because I'm leaving tomorrow."

Again, he gazed at her in a way that prohibited her from knowing what he was thinking. "Seems to me that's all the more reason to talk about it."

"But it's pointless," she said. She deliberately left the *it* vague. The conversation he wanted to have was pointless. What had happened in the laundry room was pointless. Whatever might be happening between them beyond that was pointless. She was going home to Boston tomorrow. She would be trying the biggest case of her career next week. Her life would be in upheaval after that. She wouldn't have time for conversations about anything, let alone for pursuing a relationship with Chance that wasn't going to go anywhere, anyway. A thousand miles would separate them after tomorrow. Even without the geographic distance, there was a chasm of time and experience and culture.

Reality, she made herself admit. That was what really lay between them. They came from two entirely different worlds and claimed entirely different lifestyles. Her time in Endicott had been a nice little diversion, but it wasn't real life. Not her real life. And Chance had deep roots in this community. There was no way he could be happy anywhere else. The children, too, were better off here, where they could start their lives anew and not be burdened by memories of their lost parents or the strains that came with the hectic pace of city life.

"You know, maybe it is pointless," Chance agreed. And she was surprised how much it bothered her that he did. Then he qualified, "*Maybe*. But it isn't meaningless."

No. It certainly wasn't that.

"What happened this afternoon," she said, "it happened. We can't pretend it didn't. And we can't take it back."

"But?"

"But there's no sense going forward with it, either."

The moment she said it, she regretted it. Not just because, deep down, she didn't believe it was necessarily true. But also because the look on Chance's face then was very easy to read. He was hurt. She'd done that to him. And there was no way for her to undo it.

He opened his mouth to reply, but a server arrived with the bottle of wine Felix had sent out for them and launched into a good-natured description of what it was and why they would like it, and how they'd chosen their dinner selections wisely, and… And then Poppy stopped listening, because Chance was talking to the waiter like they were old friends—which they probably were—and it felt as if that was the end of their conversation about what had happened that afternoon.

Which, she told herself, was exactly what she wanted, so why did she suddenly feel as if the entire world was collapsing around her?

It didn't help that they spent the rest of dinner talking about everything except what had happened that afternoon. Again, Poppy reminded herself that that was for the best, but again, her reminder did nothing to make her feel better. Neither did the realization that her time with Chance was drawing to a close, and this was probably the last time she would see him without the children around, and dinner was just flying by so fast, and *dammit*, why couldn't time slow down just once, just long enough for her to *enjoy* something in her life?

And then Felix was back, asking how Poppy had liked everything, and then he and Chance were arguing about the check, which Felix refused to send out—clearly, it was an old argument and one Chance regularly lost—and then they were outside, walking to his car, and the town was enclosing them like a warm embrace.

La Mariposa was one of several attached storefronts in Old Town Endicott, and as they made their way along the walk, she could see the moon hanging high overhead, threaded by wisps of white clouds and surrounded by a scattering of stars. The breeze ruffled the trees, accompanied by the soft murmur of music from another business. There were dozens of other people out enjoying the evening, but Poppy and Chance might as well have been the only two people in the world. When they reached his car, he opened the door for her and she climbed inside, and then he circled the front to the driver's side. He started the engine, but didn't put it into gear. Instead, he looked over at her.

"I don't want to go home," he said simply.

She didn't know what to say. So she just said what she knew was true in that moment. "I don't, either." And she tried not to think about how he was talking about his home here in Endicott, but she was talking about hers in Boston.

He smiled at that, albeit a little sadly. "I could

give you the grand tour. Show you everything in Endicott you haven't seen yet."

"There are things in Endicott I haven't seen yet?" she asked.

His face was the personification of the word *pshaw*. "Oh, yeah. Tons of stuff. Petrovic Library, named after our famous Arctic explorer. The barn on the Huckleberry Farm that was once a stop on the Underground Railroad. The Roxy Theater, where they still have midnight showings of *The Room* every Saturday. Deb's Downtown Diner, where Andy Warhol once ate lunch and sketched a saltshaker on a beverage napkin for a tip. The—"

"Stop," Poppy interrupted with a laugh. "I didn't realize what a hotbed of historical and cultural significance Endicott is."

Chance laughed, too, and it went a long way toward dispelling the tension that had started to settle between them. "But wait—there's more," he said in his best infomercial voice. "There's the neighborhood where I had my paper route when I was ten. The dead oak tree in Kickapoo Park where we used to hang out when we cut class. My old high school. My old middle school. My old elemen—"

"Okay, okay," Poppy surrendered with another laugh. "I give up. Give me the grand tour."

"You won't be sorry."

He threw the car into gear and steered them into

the night, showing her every site he'd promised and then some. They ended the tour at a place he called The Meadow, a few miles outside of town. Poppy wondered how a big empty space of land could be as significant as a diner with a framed beverage napkin signed by a famous artist, but the minute Chance put the car into Park and turned off the engine and headlights, she saw why. Because it was illuminated by thousands and thousands and *thousands* of fireflies dancing over the velvety black darkness.

"Oh, my," she whispered reverently when she saw them.

"Yeah, they've been putting on shows nightly every summer since I was a kid. My dad discovered this place when he was a teenager, and my folks used to bring me and Logan out here so we could watch them. I'm honestly not sure how many people in Endicott even know about it. Those of us who do don't want to share it. If too many people found out, the traffic might chase off the fireflies."

Poppy had seen a lot of beautiful things in her life. Artwork at the Louvre. Broadway extravaganzas. European mountain ranges. Asian marketplaces. Felix Suarez's paella. But she'd never ever seen anything as beautiful as a silken night shimmering with living luminescence. She turned to look at Chance. Oh, wait. She had seen something even more beautiful than this. Chance Foley looking at her the way he was looking at her now.

How was she going to leave this man behind? How would she ever be able to live a life that didn't have him in it?

Instead of looking for answers to those questions, she leaned forward, curled her hand over his cheek and kissed him. Kissed him as if she would never see him again. Because she wouldn't. Not like this. Even when their paths crossed again in the future, it would be in another place and another time. It would never be like this again.

He kissed her back immediately, even went so far as to unsnap both of their seat belts before taking her into his arms. But where their embrace that afternoon had been unexpected, explosive and uncontrolled, their kisses now were thoughtful, slow and methodical.

And very, very arousing.

Poppy threaded the fingers of one hand into his hair and curled the others into his shirt, and he, in turn, pulled her closer. For long moments, they only held each other and kissed, deeper and deeper and deeper still until he pushed back his seat as far as it would go and pulled her completely into his lap. She looped her arms around his neck, and he cupped a hand on her hip, and they settled in for a nice long session of necking. Every time their mouths touched, her heart rate quickened, and every time he traced his hands over her hips and back and ribs, she wanted more. When he lifted a hand to the top button of her dress, she dropped one of hers to his shirt. Together, they unfastened each other's garments and shoved them aside.

When Chance saw what she had on beneath, he grinned. "Oh, I was so hoping I'd get to see these while you were here," he said of the black lacy undergarments.

He ran a hand over the translucent fabric covering her breast, dragging his thumb over its peak. Poppy groaned in response, wishing they had a little more room so that she could touch him as intimately.

He stroked her again. "I just wish I could see them a little better."

"Not much opportunity for that in here," she said with regret. "But maybe—"

Maybe what? she asked herself. This was an impossible situation in more ways than one. They couldn't make love in Chance's car. Well, they could, but it probably wasn't a good idea, even on what was promising to be a completely deserted road. And trying to make love at his house would fill her, at least, with apprehension at having the children so close. Yes, people made love under the same roof as their kids all the time. But Poppy never had. She wasn't comfortable with the idea of doing so now.

"I have a confession to make," he said suddenly, his voice a warm whisper by her ear. "When I went out to get a haircut this afternoon, I, um… I sort of arranged for us to get a room tonight at the Blue Moon Motor Inn, a few more miles up the road."

She pulled back to look at him, her eyes narrowed. "Presumptuous much?"

He grinned with a mix of hopefulness and confidence that made her hot all over again. "Look, it was just in case."

"Just in case what?"

"Just in case we ended up exactly as we are right now."

He dragged the backs of his knuckles over her breast, making her cry out softly. Okay, so he had a point. Maybe he wasn't so much presumptuous as he was prepared. Then another thought occurred to her. "Wait a minute. How did you get a room? This town was booked solid, last I checked."

"Funny story," Chance told her. "Josh Cromarty, the Blue Moon manager, is a high-school friend. Well, acquaintance. Anyway, his family has owned the place for generations, and back in high school, it was a well-known secret that Josh always made it look like Room 21 was reserved for the night on the books, so his parents wouldn't give it to anyone else, when in fact, it was always vacant. He would then auction off the key to it to the highest bidder on any given night."

"Resourceful," Poppy said.

"Yeah, he paid his way through college with the proceeds. Anyway, now that he runs the motel himself, it's no secret that he still keeps Room 21 vacant, and he still auctions it off on any given night."

Noting her vaguely horrified response, he hurried on, "Not to high-school kids, because that would be inappropriate and gross, not to mention probably illegal. These days, it's to adults who... Let's just say to people who wouldn't want their spouses or significant others to find out they have a little something going on on the side."

"You realize, of course, that that's still inappropriate and gross," Poppy said.

"But not illegal. Besides, I've never used Josh's services before."

She eyed him skeptically.

"Okay, Glenna MacAfee and I won the room a couple times our senior year."

She continued to eye him skeptically.

"All right, fine. Once, a few years after that, too, when Glenna came home from Purdue at Thanksgiving. Her parents didn't approve of me. But that's it."

Poppy wanted to think badly of Chance for his illicit trysts in the past, but really, all she could think about was how Glenna MacAfee was a lucky girl who had stupid parents.

"Anyway," he said again, "this afternoon, I placed a bid on Room 21, and I won tonight's auction."

Poppy said nothing to that. Mostly because what she wanted very badly to say was *yes*.

"I told Lilah we might be out pretty late," he added in reference to Max's sister, who was sitting the kids.

Still, Poppy said nothing. But she lifted a hand to his face, tracing her fingers along the elegant ridge of his cheekbone.

"She said we could stay out as late as we wanted, 'cause she'll be up late working on her thesis, anyway."

Poppy remained silent. But she skimmed her hand to his jaw, pulling her thumb along its powerful line.

"I think it's more, though, because she wants to tell Max how you and I stayed out really, really late."

Poppy remained mute. But she moved her hand to the strong column of his throat, curling her fingers over his nape.

"So you and I should probably, you know, stay out really, really, *really* late."

"Yes," Poppy finally said softly. Seductively. With certainty. "Yes, we should."

Evidently that was all Chance needed to hear, because after another swift kiss, he gently returned her to her seat and started the car again. Then he threw it into gear, and they were on the road once more, heading even farther away from town. A million things scrambled through Poppy's head as they drove, but nothing settled long enough for her to focus on any of them. Her senses, though, were working overtime, and everything she felt, she felt keenly. The warm rush of the night air on her face as it swept through the window, the sweet aroma of honeysuckle filling her nose, the hum of the tires along the highway seeming to say, *Faster, faster, faster.* And then the blue-and-green neon sign of the motel came into view, and then they were parking in front of Room 21, and then Chance was fumbling with the key, and then they were inside, and after that…

After that, Poppy stopped thinking at all. There was only Chance and her and the too-few hours they had left together. And Chance was, in that moment, what she wanted more than anything in the world. The only thing she wanted. Everything she wanted.

A single lamp burned in the corner of the room, casting a soft golden glow over the furnishings and decor that probably hadn't changed since the place

opened in the mid-twentieth century. Chance closed
the door behind them and pulled her into his arms,
covering her mouth with his. As he unbuttoned her
dress, she unbuttoned his shirt and pants, until all
of those garments were pooled at their feet. For the
first time, she had unlimited access to all that skin
and muscle, and she took advantage, touching every
exposed inch of him. He was hot and solid and alive
beneath her fingertips, and if she could just spend
the rest of her life touching him, she would die a
happy woman. But he obviously had other plans,
because slowly, slowly, oh…so slowly, he began
backing her toward the already-turned-down bed.
Josh Cromarty evidently knew his guests in Room
21 would always have other things on their minds.

Chance pulled his mouth from hers and gazed
down at the black lingerie he'd only enjoyed hints
of before. He touched the pearls encircling her neck.
"You are so beautiful," he told her.

Poppy dropped her gaze to take in all of him,
save what his paisley boxers—wow, they looked
brand-new—still covered. "You're not so bad yourself."

She smiled. Chance smiled. Then he dipped a
finger beneath the strap of her bra and pushed it
over her shoulder. He did the same with the other
strap. So Poppy reached behind herself and un-
hooked the garment, letting it, too, fall to the floor.

He uttered a wild little sound at seeing her. Then he dropped to the edge of the bed and pulled her into his lap, straddling him. Without hesitating, he moved his mouth to her breast to cover its sensitive peak and tasted her deeply, again and again and again. Poppy cried out at the contact, weaving her fingers tightly into his hair, riding out wave after wave of sensation. When she moved her other hand between their legs and caressed him through the fabric of his boxers, he nipped her skin lightly, then turned them so that they lay alongside each other on the bed.

As he continued to minister to her breast, he pushed a hand into her panties and buried his fingers in the hot wet core of her, stroking her softly before inserting one long finger inside her. She gasped at the intrusion, but bucked her hips against him, drawing him even deeper inside. Then she dipped her hand beneath his waistband to run her fingers along the powerful length of him, palming the damp head. That was when they pulled away from each other long enough to remove what was left of their clothing. But when Poppy reached for her pearls, Chance stayed her hand.

"No, leave the pearls on," he said breathlessly. "But just the pearls."

She smiled. "Really?"

"Oh, yeah."

Aunt Theodora would be so proud, she thought as she reached for the bedside lamp.

"No, leave that on, too," Chance said. "I want to see you."

She wanted to see him, too. All of him. She got her wish when he rolled over to open the drawer of the other nightstand—his backside was as gorgeous as his front—from which he withdrew a condom that he hastily began to open. Wow. Josh Cromarty really did know how to show his guests a good time. Then Chance was pulling Poppy into his arms again, kissing her and touching her again. And again. And again. And again. And then he was bracing his arms on each side of her as he entered her, and she was circling her legs around his waist to pull him in deeper still. And then she was on top, lunging down on him. And then she was on her hands and knees with him behind her, thrusting harder and harder against her, until they both cried out their completion.

They tumbled back onto the mattress, clinging to each other, breathing as if neither would ever have enough oxygen again.

For a long moment, they only looked at each other. Poppy traced his features with light fingers as he brushed his curled knuckles between her breasts.

"I wish you didn't have to leave tomorrow," he said.

So did Poppy. But she didn't tell him that.

"I wish you could stay longer."

So did she. But she didn't tell him that, either.

When she didn't reply, he moved his hand to her face, tracing the line of her jaw to her temple, then weaving his fingers into her hair, then curling them around her nape. A frisson of electricity followed everywhere he touched her, then down her spinal cord to join with the heat still shimmering between her legs. She already wanted him again. She wondered if there would ever come a day when she stopped wanting him.

"This week has just been…" He inhaled deeply and exhaled on a long incredulous breath. "It's not been like anything I've ever experienced in my life."

"I would imagine not," she said softly, opening her hand over his warm chest, loving the steady thump, thump, thump of his heart beneath her fingertips. "It's not every day that someone inherits two kids overnight."

He met her gaze levelly. "I wasn't talking about the kids."

A bubble of something warm and joyful rose inside her, lodging in her chest, very near her heart. Her icy, ruthless, cutthroat heart, so traitorous at the moment for being none of those things.

But she said nothing in response to Chance's confession. She couldn't. All she could think about was how this week hadn't been like anything she'd ever experienced, either. And it was all because of him. She'd just never met a man like him. Had never known men like him existed. She'd never realized how much she wanted someone like him in her life. But to say things like that made them real. And they couldn't be real. Men like Chance weren't a part of her life. Not her real life in Boston. He belonged here, in this place of friendly people and gentle living. He belonged where things moved slower and more softly. A world absent of indifferent families and icy, ruthless cutthroats.

When she still said nothing, he continued, "The mornings when I've woken up and come into the kitchen for coffee, and I've seen you out on the patio, working in your pajamas, it's like… It's weird, Poppy, but it feels like you've always been there. Like I've always woken up that way in the morning. And I like it. I like seeing you sitting out there, working." He grinned. "In one of my shirts. And I like sitting out there, talking with you before the kids wake up. I like sitting out there with you at night, too. It just feels… I don't know. Right. Like that's how things should always be. It's like the whole universe has just fallen into place around me this week. I never realized how out of whack everything was until you and the kids showed up. And now…"

With every word he spoke, Poppy grew more distressed. Because this week had felt strangely right to her, too. And it wasn't. It wasn't right at all.

"We should get...back," she said softly, forcing herself to say *back* instead of *home*, because she had to stop thinking of Chance's house that way.

He looked a little crestfallen. "But I thought we were going to stay out really, really, *really* late."

"It is late," she told him. And it was. It was too late. Too late to take back too many things she never should have said or done. "We should get...back."

"Okay," he told her. "If that's what you want."

It wasn't what she wanted. But, like so many other things in her life, it was what she had to do, whether she liked it or not.

When she said nothing, Chance told her, "Okay. Then we'll go home."

Chapter Twelve

Had someone told Chance a couple of weeks ago that he would have to master the art of making pancakes with two six-year-olds while a yapping puppy nipped at their feet, he would have thought that person delusional. But here he was in his kitchen, early on a Thursday morning, doing exactly that. As Finn stirred a bowl of pancake batter that, even to Chance's untrained eye, looked way too thin to make anything more than a mess, Quinn dumped half a bag of chocolate chips into it. He was going to go out on a limb and say this wasn't exactly the kind of breakfast Poppy normally consumed. But the kids had insisted they needed to make her breakfast in bed for her last day in Endicott before she returned to Boston.

Then again, this whole week probably hadn't been anywhere close to Poppy's sort of normal. And maybe, if he and the kids did this thing right, he could show her once and for all how the life she had here—as short as it had been so far—was the one to which she was better suited. *Icy, ruthless, cut-throat attorney*, he repeated to himself. How many times had she assured him this week that that was what she was? Attorney, sure. But more like cheery, harmless cream puff.

On any other day, she would have been up and at work out on the patio by now. But after the late hours—and, ah, other parts—of last night, she hadn't yet stirred. If they didn't get a move on, though, they were going to miss their window of opportunity.

"I think they need more chocolate chips," Finn said as he stirred some of the batter over the top of the bowl and onto the floor—where Pippi promptly cleaned it up with her tongue.

"Or maybe some raisins," Quinn said. "Uncle Chance, do we have any raisins?"

We, Chance couldn't help noting his niece had said. She'd asked if *we* had them, not *you*, which was how she'd asked for everything else this week, unless it was something that had come down from

Boston with her. She was thinking about this house as their house now, not his. It was a good sign. He just wished there were someone else who might consider that a possibility, too.

"I'm afraid we do not have raisins," he said. "But I'll put them on the grocery list. And I think there are plenty of chocolate chips in there," he added when he saw Finn going for the bag in Quinn's hand. "It's time to heat up the pan."

It would have been better if they had a griddle. Or, you know, a bigger frying pan than the one he'd always used for the handful of things he made in a frying pan for one person. His kitchen was so poorly equipped to handle a family. Why was his kitchen so poorly equipped for that? Even single people he knew had a full set of cookware and appliances that did more than brew coffee or toast bread. He could have at least had more than a few mismatched pans and scant utensils. Some family man he was turning out to be.

Then again, family didn't come down to how well equipped the kitchen was, did it? It came down to how well equipped the heart was. And although his kitchen could use some pumping up to accommodate him and the kids in the future, his heart was doing just fine. The kids had helped a lot with that. But Poppy had helped even more.

Surprise, surprise—Chance liked being a family man. More, even, than when he'd been part of a family before. Maybe because, when he was a kid, he hadn't fully understood what family meant or how important it was to have one. Sure, he'd built a family of sorts with Felix and Max and their families, but Felix's and Max's families had always been, well, Felix's and Max's. They'd led their own lives and done their own things and had gotten together when it suited them. Sometimes Chance had been with them, but more often, he hadn't. But real family… Real family was there for you 24/7, whenever you needed them. Real family had your back. Real family took care of you, and you took care of them—24/7.

He looked at the kids again. Quinn was balancing a carton of orange juice that was way too big for her six-year-old hands, and Finn was staring impatiently at the butter melting in the pan. Both were running their mouths simultaneously, but talking about the same thing—whether or not Poppy would prefer syrup or jam on the pancakes they hadn't even made yet, and did we—*we*—have any other flavor than strawberry? Chance smiled at both the kids and the mess they were making. He would have thought he would resent having his house overrun by children who left their stamp on everything in the form of various messes and awkward attempts at cleanup. Instead, his house—*their* house—felt more like a home than it ever had before.

Somehow, the three of them managed to create a dozen passably edible-looking, if somewhat mis-shapen, pancakes, three of which they piled onto a plate for Poppy, and the rest onto a plate that went into the oven for them later. Finn then poured a glass of juice, spilling only a little onto the tray, then plopped jam into a bowl and filled a coffee cup with syrup because Chance didn't even have a pitcher. Hell, the only reason he had a tray was to carry things in from the grill to the kitchen. Quinn ran outside to collect a handful of wild violets that dotted the backyard, which she dropped into a glass of water and placed amid everything else.

Chance shook his head at the tray as he lifted it to carry upstairs. What the kids lacked in tidiness, they made up for in enthusiasm. He only hoped Poppy appreciated all the work they'd put into her last meal in Endicott.

Something unpleasant bubbled up inside him at the realization of that. In a matter of hours, they'd be dropping her off at the airport in Louisville—and they'd get her there on time, because they were going to leave super early—and waving farewell to her from the we're-staying-here side of security. Chance knew the airport well. It was impossible to see anyone once they passed through those gates.

Once she was through security, she'd be well and truly gone. And something about that realization caused something inside him to shift in a way that didn't feel right at all.

He pushed the thought, and the feeling, away. Right now, they had a breakfast to serve.

The children danced around him as he ascended the stairs, nearly making him drop the tray more than once. Then, giggling softly and shushing each other, they pushed open the door to Poppy's bedroom. His bedroom. Their bedroom. Whatever.

When he saw that she was already up, sitting in bed with her tablet in her lap, he knew she wasn't going to be surprised by their appearance. She must have awoken earlier, heard their ruckus in the kitchen and suspected what was up. But she'd stayed put where she was so as not to ruin the children's surprise. Now she feigned being so engrossed in whatever she was doing that she didn't hear them come in, despite the kids being about as subtle as a herd of stampeding wildebeests. Her short hair was sticking up from sleep, and her glasses were perched on the edge of her nose, and Chance didn't think he'd ever seen her looking more beautiful. He was suddenly hit by wave after wave of what they had enjoyed the night before, and god help him, in that moment, he wanted her again. Desperately.

Thankfully, the children shouted, "Surprise!" and

launched themselves onto the bed. Poppy looked up, doing a damned fine job of being startled by their appearance, smiling with delight as she gathered them close and placed a kiss at the crown of each dark head. Then she looked at Chance. She was less convincing in her reaction to him, struggling to look as if nothing had changed since the day before when, in fact—for him, at least—the entire world had been shuffled and swayed.

Before either of them could say a word, Quinn announced, "We made you breakfast in bed."

"So I see," Poppy replied as she set her tablet onto the nightstand.

Chance approached slowly, telling himself it was because he didn't want to spill anything, and not because he just wasn't sure what his reception from Poppy was going to be this morning. Last night…

Damn. Last night, neither of them had been thinking about this morning. Or later today. Or next week. Or next year. Or anything else. Maybe, in hindsight, that hadn't been such a good idea. Especially with the realization that the presence of two children this morning—and later today and next week and next year—would prohibit them from talking about what, exactly, *had* happened last night and why it had happened the way it did. At the time, what they'd done had felt like the most natural thing in the world. It had felt like something destined. Something normal. Something right. Now, though...

"Good morning," he said when he reached the bed.

The children scrambled out of the way enough that he could set the tray beside Poppy. When he looked up, she was smiling down at her breakfast of spilled juice, tepid coffee, crushed violets and pancakes the color of wet dirt. Then she looked at the kids. And she looked at Chance. And she smiled. A smile that took his breath away. Because it was so genuinely, unabashedly happy.

"This is the best breakfast I've ever seen," she told them. "No one has ever brought me breakfast in bed before."

For some reason, that heartened Chance. He liked that he was the first guy to do something like this for her. Before he could stop himself, he told her, "You should have someone bringing you breakfast in bed every morning."

Her smile faltered some at that, but she rallied. Mostly. "I don't usually eat breakfast," she said as she reached for her fork. "Unless maybe it's a bagel or muffin or something from the break room at work. Even then, I usually don't have time."

Finn said, "But, Poppy, it's the most important meal of the day!"

"So I've heard."

She splashed a little syrup onto the pancake and cut a modest chunk of it with her fork. Then, after only a small hesitation, she popped it into her mouth. Wow. She deserved an Academy Award for looking so enraptured by the taste.

"Delicious," she told the children, reaching for her tepid coffee to wash it down.

"We'll make pancakes for you every time you come to visit," Quinn told her earnestly.

"Yeah," Finn agreed. "When are you coming back?"

Poppy's gaze flew to Chance's. He only shook his head imperceptibly. She was on her own with this one. He wanted to hear the answer to that question himself.

She sipped her coffee carefully, then placed it back on the tray. "Well," she said as she fork-cut another piece of the pancake. "I'm not sure."

The children's expressions dampened. They looked at each other, then at Chance. All he could do was shrug. But he did his best to help.

"Poppy is super busy," he reminded them. "She has that big case coming up, and then probably another one after that, and probably another one after that."

The kids looked back at her. "Is that true?" Finn asked.

Poppy was chewing another bite of pancake, so she only nodded.

"But Thanksgiving is in November," Quinn said. "You can come visit us for Thanksgiving, right?"

Poppy swallowed. "I don't know, sweetie. That's too far away for me to be sure."

"Then Christmas," Finn said. "You have to come for Christmas."

She was clearly growing more and more uncomfortable. Chance didn't want to hang her out to dry. But he didn't see any reason to make things easy, either. She was the one who kept insisting how important her job and life in Boston were. If that was true, she could explain it to the kids in a way they'd understand. And then maybe he would understand it, too.

"I don't know," she said again. She brightened. "But maybe you guys could come to Boston to visit me for Thanksgiving or Christmas."

The kids seemed to like that idea. "We could do that Pilgrim Thanksgiving thing!" Quinn said excitedly. "Like we did with Mommy and Daddy last year."

"And go to the aquarium!" Finn added.

"And ride on the trolley!"

"And go to a Bruins game!"

"And see *The Nutcracker*!"

The children rattled off easily a dozen things to

do on their prospective trips to Boston. And with each one, Poppy looked a little more panicked. Chance knew it was because she was thinking she'd never have the time to devote to those things. She'd be too busy at the office, being icy, ruthless and cutthroat.

But all she said to the children was "Well, we'll see."

She seemed to have a little trouble finishing her breakfast after that, but the kids didn't seem to notice. They were too busy planning the next time they saw Poppy, whether it was here in Endicott or up on her turf. They were so excited about it Chance didn't want to spoil their fun. There were months between now and the holidays. By then, it shouldn't be that difficult for him to figure out how to explain to the kids in a way they would understand why Poppy wouldn't be making it back to Endicott anytime soon. Explain it to them, anyway. He wasn't sure he'd ever understand that himself.

Her flight would be leaving at a little after two o'clock. So once she finished breakfast, Chance and the kids retreated to the kitchen to have their own and then clean up their mess while she got ready and packed her things. Later, they ate a quick lunch together—in Louisville, since Chance hadn't wanted to risk making Poppy miss her flight again by spending any more time in Endicott than they had to—and then he fulfilled the promise he'd made to the kids the day he met them. He took them to Muth's for a bag of Modjeskas each. He bought a bag for Poppy, too, to take back as a memento, however temporary.

"I don't care how big and busy and cosmopolitan Boston is," he told her as he handed over the little white bag. "I bet you can't get Modjeskas there."

"You can get anything in Boston," she told him. But there was something in her voice that sounded sad and far away.

"Not like these you can't," he assured her. "These are the real thing."

Her gaze met his, and then she looked at the kids. Chance would have thought they'd be halfway into their bags of candy by now; however, they hadn't yet touched them. Instead, they were watching him and Poppy. And they were doing it with an awareness that seemed way beyond their years.

"I'm going to miss you guys," she said to the children.

As one, they ran to her and threw their arms around her. But they didn't beg her to stay as they had before. Maybe because they were more comfortable with Chance now. Maybe because they were confident of her return. Either way, it was a good sign.

"We'll miss you, too," Quinn said with just a small sniffle.

"But we'll see you soon," Finn added, sounding pretty sure of himself.

Chance was sure they'd all see Poppy in the not-too-distant future, too. He just wished it would be under circumstances that were different from the ones they seemed bound to be.

Poppy looked at Chance. "I'll miss you, too."

He nodded. But all he said was "We should probably get going."

Since it was the middle of the day, the airport wasn't especially busy. That meant Poppy got checked in quickly and that the line at security was pretty short. *Dammit.* She gathered the children close one last time and gave them each big hugs and kisses. Then she stood and looked at Chance.

He had never experienced a more awkward moment in his life. What was he supposed to say? *See ya? Have a great flight? Catch you on the flip side?* What was he supposed to do? Extend his hand for a shake? Lift it to his forehead in a cocky salute? Wiggle his fingers in farewell? Especially when what he wanted to do was bend her backward for the most intense Hollywood kiss he could manage.

Poppy saved him the trouble of figuring it all out by simply saying, "I'll be in touch."

Wow. She was already reverting back to the attorney thing. She even managed to adopt the icy, ruthless, cutthroat shell pretty well. That was all it was, though, Chance knew—a shell. No way did he believe it had ever been an actual part of her.

"Yeah, I won't be too hard to find," he told her.

She grabbed the handle of her carry-on and adjusted the strap of her briefcase on her shoulder. "Well, then," she said.

"Well, then," he replied.

"Thanks for everything."

"You're welcome. Thank you for everything."

"You're welcome."

"Have a safe flight."

"Thanks."

"Text me when you get there."

"I will."

Boy, if this was a Hollywood film, it wasn't going to win any Oscars for best screenplay. That Hollywood kiss was going to be totally out of the question. But that didn't mean he couldn't kiss her goodbye. Impulsively, he leaned forward and quickly brushed his lips over her cheek. When he pulled back, he was surprised to see she had closed her eyes, as if he really had bent her backward and laid one on her.

He couldn't bring himself to say goodbye. So he told her, "See you, Poppy Digby. Good luck with your case next week."

His reminder of her case must have triggered something in her brain, because when she opened her eyes, the attorney appeared to be back. She straightened, gripped her bags more forcefully and nodded once.

But all she said was "Thanks."

Then she was moving into the security line that was even shorter than it had been before and was moving way too fast. She flashed her ID and boarding pass at the guard and fell into the line he indicated. She tugged off her shoes and placed them into the bin with her briefcase, then settled the carry-on on the conveyor belt behind them. She passed through the body scanner, lifting her arms dutifully over her head, then exited it to collect her things at the other end. Not once did she look back at Chance or the kids. Not once did she lift a hand in farewell. Not once did she indicate there were other people seeing her off.

She was already back to considering herself alone, Chance thought. Already convincing herself she didn't belong here with them.

Well, good luck with that, Poppy Digby, he thought. *Good expletive-deleted-because-there-are-children-present luck with that.*

Chapter Thirteen

Poppy's parents' town house in Beacon Hill had been in the family since it was built in 1838. It had hosted, she was certain, hundreds, perhaps thousands, of magnificent social events in its day. But none of them could have been nearly as magnificent as the Congratulations, Poppy! extravaganza that was in full swing tonight. Because Poppy had won her big case two weeks ago, and her firm had offered a full partnership days later.

In their ecstatic relief that their daughter was finally, *finally* suitable enough material to join the ranks of all the Digbys who'd come before her, Edgar and Delilah Digby had spared no expense.

There were exquisite food and drink, a string quartet and a guest list that included captains of industry, entertainment VIPs and at least two senators.

All in all, it was a gorgeous, glittering gala. So why did Poppy feel so gloomy? Dressed in an off-the-shoulder silk cocktail dress of bright coral— she must have been channeling Quinn Foley when she bought it, because she couldn't think of a single other reason why she would have gravitated toward it—she leaned in the doorway of the butler's pantry that joined the kitchen to the great room, gripping a cocktail she'd been nursing all evening. She'd had to escape the throngs of well-wishers in the room beyond, because the incessant barrage of congratulations and attagirls had begun to ring hollow, to the point where she was starting to feel like an absolute fraud.

Her feelings made no sense. She'd achieved the thing she'd been working herself to near-death for for a decade. She could write her own ticket for whatever future she envisioned for herself. She deserved every compliment she'd received tonight. But her massive achievement didn't feel like an achievement at all. In fact, none of the accomplishments she'd won over the years felt like accomplishments tonight. Instead of feeling buoyed by her successes, she felt as if she were drowning. The thing she had been so sure she wanted more than anything felt instead like nothing at all.

"What are you hiding from?"

Poppy turned to find her mother gliding up behind her from the kitchen, cradling a glass of champagne. Poppy's sister and brother trailed behind her. Ever the society grande dame, even when she was also a full-time attorney, Delilah Digby looked chic and confident this evening in a simple long-sleeved dress of midnight blue velvet, her silver hair twisted into a perfect chignon. Odette was a younger version of their mother, right down to the dress style—though she'd opted for a racier amethyst. Barnaby's dark blue suit and plum necktie were the perfect complement. The levels of champagne in her siblings' glasses were identical to her mother's, because one thing her two older siblings had mastered was keeping perfect pace with their parents. It was something that had allowed the four other members of her family to bond so perfectly. Not for the first time, Poppy wondered how she could come from the same gene pool.

"I'm not hiding," she lied.

"Well, you're certainly not circulating," her mother pointed out.

"I've been circulating all night. I need a break."

"Translation, *I'm hiding*," her mother said with disapproval.

"Oh, leave her alone, Mother," Odette said. "At least she's trying."

Barnaby chimed in, "Yes, it's not every day Poppy can celebrate her successes, is it?"

Only Odette and Barnaby could make words of encouragement sound so discouraging.

"I still can't imagine what you were thinking when you bought that dress," her mother said. "At that awful used clothing store, too."

"Vintage," Poppy corrected her. "It was a vintage clothing store. It's a vintage dress. Christian Dior, in fact. It's probably something you would have worn yourself forty or fifty years ago."

"Not in that color, I wouldn't," her mother assured her.

"I think I look pretty," Poppy said, echoing what Quinn had told her that day in Endicott. And she remembered, too, what Chance had said not long after. A curl of heat unwound in her midsection at the memory. There was a time when she would have wanted to kick a man for calling her pretty. She'd worked too hard to be considered pretty. But when Chance had let her know he thought she was pretty, she'd felt weirdly, wildly happy.

"You do look pretty," her mother conceded. "But wouldn't you rather look professional?"

A few months ago, Poppy would have said yes. But then, a few months ago, she never would have put on a dress like this to begin with. The thought of looking pretty would have horrified her. Then having a six-year-old girl tell her she looked pretty had felt kind of sweet. And having Chance reiterate the compliment…

Well…that had gone beyond feeling sweet. That had felt incandescent.

"You know, it's possible to be pretty *and* professional," Poppy told her mother. "It's not like women can only be one or the other."

"No, dear, that's exactly how it is," her mother replied. "Especially at your level of success. You need to think about these things now that you've *finally* made it to the upper echelons."

"That either-or business is a construct of the patriarchy," Poppy countered, knowing constructs of the patriarchy were some of her mother's favorite targets.

But her mother surprised her. "No, Poppy, it's a fact of life. And it was created by and is perpetuated by men and women both."

"Sucks to be you," Barnaby said with a swallow of champagne.

To her credit, Odette stiffened at their brother's comment. Then she ruined it by saying, "Even if there is a double standard, we have to abide by it if we want to be the best version of ourselves."

Meaning the most successful version of themselves, Poppy knew. And what a load of crap, saying women had to tolerate intolerance in order to get through life. "That's not very progressive thinking," she said.

"Digbys aren't very progressive creatures," her mother replied.

Which was true. No family came into massive wealth and power and stayed there by challenging the status quo that gave them the massive wealth and power to begin with. Especially families as wealthy and powerful as the Digbys. Poppy was both a spawn of that status quo and one of its citizens. This was the world she was born into and the one she would be moving in for the rest of her life. The last thing she should be thinking about was trying to shake things up.

"You're one of us now, dear," her mother said, as if reading her mind. "Your father and I are so proud of you."

Poppy felt a wave of nausea roll through her belly. Not only because her mother had just indicated it was her professional success that made her a member of the family, when one would think that was due to…oh, Poppy didn't know…being loved by its other members. But because, looking at her mother now, then at her siblings, then out at the great room, where so many other distinguished members of her clan were circulating in all their finery, Poppy realized this was the last place on earth she wanted to be.

"Family is important, dear," her mother said. "Never forget that."

Family was important, Poppy knew. Family was, in fact, the most important thing in the world. But as she looked out at her family—and pretty much every Digby in Boston was prowling around the Louisburg Square mansion this evening—they didn't feel like family at all.

Probably because this wasn't her family, she realized. And this wasn't her home. Her family and home were a thousand miles away, in a small town in southern Indiana where she'd spent less than a week and enjoyed herself more than she had in an entire lifetime here.

She looked down at the glass in her hand. The one that had originally held ice and a shot of very good rye whiskey. The rye had disappeared hours ago—she'd figured downing it in one gulp would go a long way toward enabling her to face her alleged family—and the ice was nearly melted. There were still a few limp pieces floating around, but they wouldn't be there for long. Soon, that ice was going to be as melted as—as the heart of a formerly icy, ruthless, cutthroat attorney.

Gee, who knew? Apparently, icy hearts could melt. The way hers was in that moment, thinking about Chance and the children and Pippi and Endicott, Indiana, and the last time in her life—the only time in her life—when she was truly, unequivocally, irreversibly happy. The only place, she knew, where she would be happy again. Because that was where her family was. And what was anyone without family?

She looked at her mother and siblings. "I gotta get outta here," she said, speaking with more conviction than she'd ever felt in her life.

"What?" her sister replied incredulously. "You can't leave your own party."

"Not the party," Poppy clarified. "Boston. I gotta get outta here."

The other Digbys, especially her mother, looked confused and horrified.

"You can't leave, sis," Barnaby said.

Her mother demanded, "Do you know how much your father and I spent on this event tonight?"

"I'm sure it was a fortune," Poppy told her. "But you know, I don't think you really threw this party for me." Before any of the Digbys could object further, she said for a third time, "I gotta get outta here."

And then she was getting out of there, fairly skipping through the kitchen before escaping through the back door. She'd left her cocktail purse and wrap locked in her car, so there really was nothing in her parents' house anymore that was hers. Honestly, in a way, nothing in their house had ever been hers. Certainly nothing she'd ever truly, deeply loved. Not the way a person was supposed to love the things—and people—they called home.

The nausea that had been fermenting in her belly all evening suddenly effervesced into a giant bubble of euphoria. Happily, Poppy headed for her car, cocktail glass with swiftly melting ice still clutched in one hand.

There was a time in his life when Sundays, to Chance, meant sleeping super late and, upon waking, doing absolutely nothing for the rest of the day. His shop was closed on Sunday, unless one of his clients had an emergency, and it was the only day of the week—at least, it used to be—when he could just take some time to be utterly, blissfully alone. Over the past month, however, he'd come to realize that Sundays were never going to be like that again. At least not until the kids were away at college. So he was gratified on this particular Sunday morning that the kids had decided, for whatever reason, to sleep in way later than usual.

Pippi, however, was another story. She came scratching at his bedroom door a little before eleven o'clock when, evidently, she couldn't rouse the kids enough to take her outside. So Chance tugged a

T-shirt on over his sweatpants and followed the puppy down the steps and out the front door. The first thing he noticed was that there was more than a touch of autumn in the air this morning, and he probably should have put on some shoes. The second thing he noticed was that Pippi was taking her sweet time getting down to business. The third thing he noticed was a yellow taxicab coming down the street.

Which was more than a little weird. With the advent of rideshares, Endicott's sole taxi service had closed up a couple of years ago, and its three drivers—all brothers who were pushing sixty— had happily cashed out and retired to Panama City. Chance couldn't remember the last time he'd seen a yellow taxicab, especially out here in the wilds of suburbia. He wondered where it was going.

Oh. His house. That was even weirder.

As it turned into his driveway, he tried to make out the occupant of the back seat. But whoever it was was on the other side and took a few minutes to pay the driver and gather their things. Then the door was opening, and a tasty brunette was climbing out, and a wave of heat was splashing through his belly, and he could hardly think straight because he was sure he must just be imagining her. But then the taxi was gone and Poppy was still there, standing in his driveway in a bright pink dress and translucent silver shawl and high heels that, even with his limited knowledge of fashion, he was pretty sure weren't normal attire for a Sunday morning. She had arrived the first time in Endicott with a carry-on and briefcase, but this time she carried only a tiny purse the same color as her shoes and…and a cocktail glass?

"Hi," she said just loudly enough for him to hear her.

"Hi," he replied just as quietly.

The two of them had exchanged texts and emails fairly regularly since her departure, all of them about the children. Their communications had been familiar and friendly, but they'd stayed within the bounds of a professional relationship. There had been no jokes or banter, no fun emojis, nothing to suggest the two of them had anything more than a polite connection cemented by the welfare of two children. Certainly, she'd said nothing about coming for a visit. And by the look of her, she hadn't done much preparing for this one.

"Ah, how's things?" Chance asked.

Seemed like a fair enough question since, judging by the look of her, things at her end might be a bit different from what she was accustomed to. A bit less icy. A little less ruthless. A tad less cutthroaty.

"Fine," she replied automatically. Then, quickly,

she backpedaled, "Well, not fine, exactly, but... better than they were."

"Oh, right," he said. "Since you won your big case a few weeks ago, I guess they made you a big-time partner in the firm. Congrats, by the way, if I never said that."

And he was pretty sure he never had. It hadn't been any kind of maliciousness or passive aggression that had caused the oversight. It was that he'd been so involved in getting the kids settled at their new school and into all their new activities—if it was Tuesday, it must be chess club and gymnastics—that he'd just lost track of the timing. He was lucky to remember his own name these days.

"Thanks," she said.

She started to say more, but Pippi recognized her and went running up to greet her, too, circling her feet and yapping happily. Poppy let out a delighted cry and knelt to pet her, setting her purse on the driveway, but never letting go of that... cocktail glass?

"She's gotten so big!" she cried with a laugh as Pippi jumped up on hind legs to cover her with kisses. "Please tell me the kids haven't changed this much."

"They haven't outgrown the clothes they brought with them yet, but by the time the weather gets really cold, a new winter wardrobe is definitely going to be in the cards."

She gave Pippi a final ear scratch, gathered up her purse and stood. A chilly morning breeze swept in from nowhere, ruffling his hair, and Poppy tugged at the thin scrap of cloth around her shoulders. She must be freezing. Some host he was.

"Come inside," he said. "I'll start the coffee."

He didn't have to tell her twice. And with every step closer she took, the heat in his belly fired hotter. It wasn't a sexual heat, though—*go figure*—but one generated by her simple nearness. It had only been weeks since he last saw her. But it felt like centuries. When she was close enough to touch, he noticed dark circles under her eyes, partly due to smudged makeup, but more due to what looked like a profound lack of sleep. Just what time had she left Boston? More to the point, *why* had she left Boston? Especially dressed the way she was and with no baggage in tow save a purse that could hold little more than her ID and a…cocktail glass?

With a softly murmured "Thank you," she preceded him into the house and to the kitchen, where she went straight to the back window. The sky was gray and cloudy, and he was pretty sure the weather people had said something about the possibility of flurries later today. If Poppy was going to stay longer than a few hours, she was going to need to go shopping again, a prospect that didn't bother him nearly as much as it had before. Or else she was going to have to swaddle up in his clothes, an idea he liked even more.

"The leaves are starting to turn," she said as she gazed out at the woods. "I see some reds and oranges."

"Sugar maples are always the first to go," Chance told her.

"I bet autumns are beautiful here."

"They are, actually."

For a long moment, she only continued to look out the window. Still clinging to her tiny purse and her...cocktail glass? Which, now that he was close enough, he could see wasn't empty, as he'd first thought. It was actually almost half-full of water.

Half-full, he repeated to himself. Not half-empty. He was taking the route of the optimist. He hoped it wasn't the wrong road.

"Poppy?" he said.

She turned around from the window to look at him, her expression a silent question mark.

He sighed softly. "Not that I'm not incredibly happy to see you, but...but what are you doing here? Dressed like that? With no luggage?"

She smiled. "I don't need luggage. Everything I need is right here."

Wow, had Chance thought that was heat in his

belly before? Because what he felt now was near explosive. Her voice had been filled with absolute conviction when she made the statement. In spite of that, he said nothing in reply. Mostly because he didn't know what to say. But also because he was afraid if he said anything, it would wake him from what was beginning to feel like a dream.

When he didn't reply, her smile fell some. "I thought Boston was home," she said. "I thought my life there was the life I was supposed to have. Because that was the only life, the only home, I ever knew. Until I came here."

Still, Chance said nothing. Because still, he was afraid to hope.

"But when I got back to Boston," she continued, "nothing felt normal. I mean, I was able to go back to my life there, but it felt like someone else's life. My apartment felt like someone else's apartment. My family—" She halted abruptly, inhaled a shaky breath and released it slowly. "The people in Boston who share my last name… They're not terrible people, but…they're not my people, either. They're not my family."

Finally, Chance found his voice. "And who are your family?" he asked, still not able to convince himself she was saying what she seemed to be saying. "Where is your home?"

"Here," she said immediately. "This is my home.

And you and the kids—" She halted again, as if she were the one afraid to hope now. "I didn't think I needed anyone," she said instead of finishing what she was going to say. "Icy, ruthless cutthroat that I am...that I was..."

She didn't finish that statement, either. Instead, she looked down at the glass in her hand, crossed the kitchen to stand before him, extending it toward him. But Chance didn't take it from her. Instead, puzzled, he only looked down into the clear liquid it held.

"See that?" she said. "That used to be ice."

He had no idea where she was going with this, so he only replied, "Okay?"

"Last night, in Boston, there was ice in this glass. But it melted."

He narrowed his eyes at her. "You brought that all the way from Boston?"

She nodded.

"They let you get on board a plane with a glass holding liquid?" he asked dubiously.

"It's less than three ounces," she told him. "And, fun fact, it's not illegal to carry glass onto a plane."

"Okay?" he repeated, still not sure what the hell they were talking about. Seriously, this had to be a dream.

"I mean, sure, they prefer you to have it wrapped up in your carry-on, but people bring glass-enclosed liquids like perfume and liquor from duty-free onto planes all the time, as long as they're less than three ounces. There was no legal precedent to prohibit me from bringing on a glass of melted ice, provided it was within the legal weight limit for liquids. I was able to argue successfully at the security gate that taking my melted ice onto the plane wasn't illegal."

Chance bit back a smile at that. "You argued a case at airport security for the legality of your possession of melted ice in a glass."

"I did," she told him. "And I won. I told you—I've never lost a case. I'm an excellent attorney."

"What time was this?"

"Four a.m."

"I see."

"They'd just opened the checkpoint. There was a line forming behind me. Surprisingly long for that time of morning."

Chance envisioned Poppy, in her short little dress and smudged makeup, holding her half-full glass, arguing with an airport security guard who was either completely exhausted at the end of their shift or nowhere near awake at the beginning. He remembered the touches of iciness, ruthlessness and cutthroatiness he'd seen in her at the end of her stay last time. He recalled all the times she'd thrown him for a loop, just by being Poppy Digby.

And he said, "Yeah, okay, I can see that."

Her smile turned smug. "They never saw what hit them."

"So I guess the question now is, why was it so important that you had to bring a glass of melted ice from Boston to Endicott?"

"Because I had to show you how it melted."

"Poppy, how long has it been since you slept?"

She took a moment to think about that. "I got a couple hours on Friday night, I think. Or was it Thursday?" She eyed him earnestly. "What day is this?"

"Sunday."

"Okay, then it was a couple hours on Thursday. I was up all night Friday on a Zoom call with some attorneys in Kyoto who are going to be very happy to not hear from me ever again."

He liked the sound of Poppy shirking her job in Boston. He didn't like that she'd only slept a couple of hours in the last three days. No wonder she wasn't making any sense. He was about to take the glass and escort her up to his room for some much-needed shut-eye, but when he reached for it, she pulled it away.

"No, you have to understand," she said. "I was standing in my parents' butler's pantry—"

He would ask later what a butler's pantry was. Right now, he wanted to see how this was going to play out.

"—and I looked down at my glass, and the ice in my drink was melting. Fast. And it made me realize that even icy, ruthless, cutthroat hearts can melt. And I thought, I don't have to be icy, ruthless and cutthroat. I can be whatever I want. I can do whatever I want. I can be wherever I want. And I realized I wanted to leave Boston. And I wanted to be here with you and Quinn and Finn. Because you know what else icy hearts can do, Chance?"

He hated that he was finding her state of exhaustion and incoherence kind of adorable. But he loved that she was having such an epiphany. "No, Poppy. I don't. What else can icy hearts do?"

"They can break. And I don't want mine to break. I just want it to melt." She held up the glass. "Like the ice. And it has." She finished her explanation with a clear and unequivocal "I love you."

Without thinking, he replied, "I love you, too."

Because he did love Poppy. He expelled a sigh that was a mixture of recognition and relief that he could finally say it out loud. The minute she'd dropped out of sight on the other side of airport security in Louisville, he'd realized he loved her. He'd probably loved her from day one. And, like an idiot, he'd let her go back to Boston without telling her. But now she was here again, telling him she was through with her life there. He wasn't going to make the same mistake twice.

There was so much they had to talk about. So many plans to make. But first, she really needed to get some sleep.

"Poppy!"

Which she could do as soon as the kids finished being delighted to see her again, because they were barreling through the kitchen door right toward her. She was probably never going to sleep again. Then again, there had been a lot of days with the kids when Chance had thought he was never going to sleep again, either. So what the hell? The two of them could never sleep again together. Forever.

Finn and Quinn hit Poppy with enough force to send her reeling. It was a minor miracle that he captured the glass in her hand before it went flying. As she tumbled to the floor with the kids to engage in furious hugging, Chance moved to pour the melted ice into the sink. Then he stopped before doing it. The twins had brought home a couple of plants from a school field trip last week, and they were still sitting on the counter. He poured half of Poppy's melted heart into one and the rest into the other. It had to be the best plant food on the planet.

He looked at the pile of people on his kitchen floor. Poppy's shoes had been kicked under the table, and she was sitting with her legs outstretched before her. Finn was on one side, Quinn on the other, and neither child looked ready to let her go anytime soon.

"We made a wish on the comet," Finn told her.

"That night after you left," Quinn said, "when Bob was up in the sky, Uncle Chance took us out in the yard to see him."

"And we wished for Bob to bring you back," Finn said.

"Forever," Quinn clarified, as if that was the most important part.

"And he did," Finn said with another hug. "Right, Poppy? You're staying forever?"

Instead of answering the children, she looked up at Chance. "Is it okay if I stay?"

He grinned. "Stay all week if you want. Stay a month. Stay forever."

Those were the words he had said to her on her first night in Endicott. He'd thought he only half meant them then. Now he was beginning to wonder if maybe Bob had had plans for all of them before Poppy even showed up. He tried to remember if he'd wished for anything else the last time Bob came to town. Because, hey, a million bucks was all well and good, but the love of someone like Poppy? A family to cherish forever? Talk about wishes come true…

Poppy grinned back. "I'd like that," she told him. "I'd like that a lot."

"Then I guess you'll just have to stay," he told her. "Forever."

Epilogue

Thanksgiving in Boston was promising to be a whirlwind, Chance was learning as he and Poppy bundled up the kids for a day that was also going to include meeting her parents and siblings and other assorted Digbys. In addition to a traditional Beacon Hill Thanksgiving feast at 7:00 p.m. sharp, they would be taking Finn and Quinn to the Turkey Trot at Franklin Park, a Festival of Lights in Attleboro and lunch at Poppy's favorite diner from high school in between. Tomorrow, he'd promised Finn and Quinn they could go to Charles Ro to check out the trains and add a few to the locomotive world they were building in the basement at home. The rest of the weekend would be filled with them seeing old friends and visiting favorite places, with a Bruins game and *The Nutcracker* thrown in for good measure.

Oh, yeah. And he and Poppy were also going to formally announce their engagement. At dinner, tonight, no less. So it was possible the traditional Beacon Hill Thanksgiving feast this year might also turn into the inaugural Cutting Off Poppy from the Family feast, too.

He told himself that wouldn't happen. He and Poppy had been living together for months, so her folks knew they were serious. And thanks to her having taken the Uniform Bar Exam a while back, she'd already been able to start practicing law in Indiana and had opened her own office in Endicott—specializing in small business law—so they knew she wasn't coming back to Massachusetts. Her hours mirrored the children's hours at school, or else the kids came to the office after school, and her receptionist—Lionel Abernathy—helped them with their homework. Though with the warm weather having come to a close, Chance's hours at the shop had dwindled to the point where he, too, was available to the kids after school most days. All in all, it was an ideal work/life balance.

And in spite of Poppy's having shacked up with the proletariat and having gone into a specialty of law her parents didn't recognize as such, they'd still invited them to come up to Boston for the holidays. Both holidays. The elder Digbys had wanted them to come for Christmas next month, too. But Chance and Poppy wanted their first Christmas with the kids—their first Christmas as a family—to be at home in Endicott. Maybe next year, they'd invite her folks down to spend the holidays with them. Maybe her folks would even accept the invitation. Hey, it could happen.

"Do we have everything?" Poppy asked as she stuffed Quinn's foot into a boot that had fitted perfectly a few weeks ago. Man, he was learning kids grew fast.

"Probably not," Chance replied. Another thing he'd learned was that it was near impossible to ever have everything you needed whenever leaving home with a child. It was even harder with two children in tow. "But it's a big city. Someone once told me you can get anything you want in Boston."

She smiled at the memory. "I meant *almost* anything. I never did find those Modjeskas anywhere in town. Or, you know, a real family. I stand corrected."

"You sure dinner tonight with your folks is a good idea?"

"No," she replied frankly. "But it's a good start." As an afterthought, she added, "Just don't tell

Mother yet that we're getting married in Endicott. And don't tell her the reception we're having here will be at the zoo."

Chance grinned devilishly. "Can I call her Mom?"

For a moment, Poppy looked horrified at the thought. From what she'd told him about her, Delilah Digby would probably spontaneously combust if someone called her *Mom*. Then Poppy smiled devilishly, too. "You know what? Yes. Call her Mom. She needs to get used to mingling with the wretched refuse like us. You can even say something like 'fudge it' or 'that's a load of crab' if you want to. That'll show her."

Chance smiled at the reminder of how much he'd altered his vocabulary to include food references since the kids moved in.

"Uncle Chance," Finn said, "you should watch your language. Those aren't nice words."

The kid said the same thing about *guacamole* and *shiitake*. Chance laughed lightly.

"You're right, Finn," he replied. "I promise to be on my best behavior tonight."

"I think we're finally ready," Poppy said. "With any luck, the snow will hold off for a few hours, at least."

"I want it to snow now," Quinn said. "I miss the snow."

So far, the only snow the kids had seen in southern Indiana had been a dusting here and there. Chance hadn't told them yet how surprisingly serious some of the snowfalls in their new home were going to be. Or how badly the town still dealt with them. He figured there probably hadn't been many school snow days in a place like Boston, which was expert at clearing the white stuff. He wanted to witness their joyful reaction to the words *There's no school today* when it first happened.

They exited their hotel room and headed for the elevator, with Finn and Quinn racing ahead of them to see who got there first to push the button. As they walked, Chance reached over and took Poppy's hand in his as if it was the most natural thing in the world to do. Because it was the most natural thing in the world to do. He was a lucky guy.

"Happy?" he asked her.

"Very," she replied.

"Think we'll have any time to ourselves this weekend?"

"I guarantee it."

He wiggled his eyebrows lasciviously. "Oh, yeah?"

She grinned back salaciously. "Yeah. Mother's had the decorator in since I moved to Endicott. I can't wait to see what she's done with the place. Especially my old room. I'm thinking you'll have to come check it out with me."

"Well, if you insist. What's her theme this time?"

"Art Deco."

"I don't know anything about Art Deco," he told her.

"Me, neither. Could take us a while to educate ourselves."

"Will the kids be okay with your folks while we're, ah, touring the house?"

She threw him a chiding look. "You're joking, right?"

"Good point. Our kids could hold their own with Vlad the Impaler."

Their gazes locked at the same time. "Our kids?" she repeated.

It was the first time either of them had used that phrase instead of *the kids* when referring to Finn and Quinn.

"Yeah, our kids," Chance echoed. It just felt right to say it. Because it was true. "Our kids. Our family. Our life. It all sounds good to me."

And it was. All good. Who would have thought a wish for a million dollars when he was fifteen would have brought something into Chance's life that was worth so much more? He sent a silent thank-you to the sky, even though Bob was long gone by now. Then he leaned in and kissed his soon-to-be wife and joined their kids at the elevator. He didn't know which of them had pushed the down button, but he smiled at the irony. As far as he was concerned, it was all going up from here.

* * * * *

If you loved Chance and Poppy,
you won't want to miss Felix's story,
Her Good-Luck Charm,
by New York Times *bestselling author*
Elizabeth Bevarly.
Available September 2022
exclusively from
Harlequin Special Edition.

Cierra's lips lifted in a smile that brightened his dark corner of the coffee shop as she straightened. "Oh, good, you remember me," she said, as if he could possibly forget her.

How could he forget Cierra Greene? Head cheerleader, class president, most popular girl in school and slayer of teenage boys' hearts.

"Yeah...I remember you." He managed to keep his voice calm even though his heart thumped as if he'd had a dozen cappuccinos.

"I was worried because you didn't return any of my calls." She tilted her head to the side and her thick, dark hair shifted. Her smile didn't go away, but there was the barest hint of accusation in her voice.

Wesley shifted in his seat. He hadn't returned her calls because ever since the day Cierra told him after a basketball game that she was ditching him for his former best friend, he'd vowed to never speak to her again. He realized vows made in high school didn't have to follow him into adulthood, but the moment he'd heard her voice message saying she'd like to meet up and talk, he'd deleted it and tried to move on with his life.

"I've been busy," he said.

"Good thing I caught you here, then, huh?" She moved to the opposite side of the table and pulled out the other chair and sat.

"How did you know I was here?"

"Mrs. Montgomery," she said, as if he should have known that one of the most respected women in town would give his whereabouts to her. She must have read the confusion on his face because she laughed, that lighthearted laugh that, unfortunately, still made his heart skip a beat. "When I couldn't reach you, my mom called around. Mrs. Montgomery said you typically spend Friday afternoons here. So, here I am!" She held out her arms and spoke as if she were a present.

Her bright smile and enthusiasm stunned him for a second. Wesley cleared his throat and took a sip of his coffee to compose himself. How many years later—fifteen—and he still had the lingering remnants of a crush on her?

Come on, Wes, you gotta do better than that!

He took a long breath and looked back at her. "Here you are."

Don't miss
The Spirit of Second Chances *by Synithia Williams,*
available September 2022 wherever
Harlequin Special Edition books and ebooks are sold.

Harlequin.com

Get 4 FREE REWARDS!

We'll send you 2 FREE Books plus 2 FREE Mystery Gifts.

FREE Value Over **$20**

Both the **Harlequin® Special Edition** and **Harlequin® Heartwarming™** series feature compelling novels filled with stories of love and strength where the bonds of friendship, family and community unite.

HARLEQUIN
PLUS

Announcing a **BRAND-NEW** multimedia subscription service for romance fans like you!

Read, Watch and Play.

Experience the easiest way to get the romance content you crave.

Start your **FREE 7 DAY TRIAL** at
<u>www.harlequinplus.com/freetrial</u>.

 **HARLEQUIN**

Heartfelt or thrilling, passionate or uplifting—Harlequin is more than just happily-ever-after.

With twelve different series to choose from and new books available every month, you are sure to find stories that will move you, uplift you, inspire and delight you.

SIGN UP FOR THE HARLEQUIN NEWSLETTER

Be the first to hear about great new reads and exciting offers!

Harlequin.com/newsletters

Love Harlequin romance?

DISCOVER.

Be the first to find out about promotions,
news and exclusive content!

f Facebook.com/HarlequinBooks

y Twitter.com/HarlequinBooks

◉ Instagram.com/HarlequinBooks

Ⓟ Pinterest.com/HarlequinBooks

YouTube YouTube.com/HarlequinBooks

ReaderService.com

EXPLORE.

Sign up for the Harlequin e-newsletter and
download a free book from any series at
TryHarlequin.com

CONNECT.

Join our Harlequin community to
share your thoughts and connect
with other romance readers!
Facebook.com/groups/HarlequinConnection

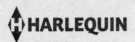